CONSORT OF PAIN

THE WITCH'S CONSORTS #3

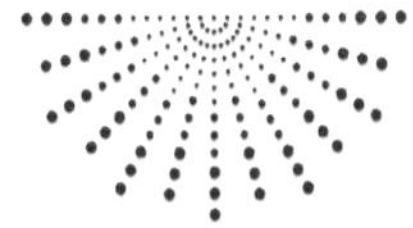

EVA CHASE

INK SPARK PRESS

Consort of Pain

Book 3 in the Witch's Consorts series

This is a work of fiction. Any resemblance to actual persons, living or dead, or actual events is purely coincidental.

First Digital Edition, 2018

Cover design: Cover Reveal Designs

Ebook ISBN: 978-1-989096-10-9

Paperback ISBN: 978-1-989096-13-0

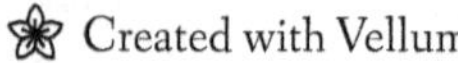 Created with Vellum

CHAPTER ONE

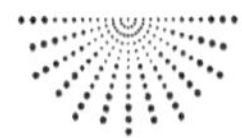

Rose

I woke up on a padded bench in a small white room, and my body immediately jerked upright, tensing to defend myself. Then I realized I couldn't have managed that even if there'd been anyone in the room to defend myself from.

Fat spongy mittens encased my hands, holding my fingers still—so I couldn't weave any magic with them. A thin but sturdy chain held my shackled wrists a few inches from each other, and my ankles were bound the same way. The chains clinked when I tugged at them, the cool shackles digging into my skin. All the usual movements I might have made to call forth a spell were closed off to me.

This room was a prison cell.

What had happened to the guys? To my consorts?

My heart lurched. Fractured memories of my last moments with the five of them swam through my head.

The Witching Assembly's enforcers had burst in so suddenly, and so many of them—I couldn't even remember what the woman who'd been leading them had looked like other than an impression of mousy brown hair. I'd whirled around, snapping my arms up in a quick magicking, but she and the other witches with her had already been hurling paralyzing spells at me. At least three of them had crashed into me at the same time, knocking me to the floor.

I *could* remember her voice, sharp and brisk as she'd informed me of my crime. *Rose Hallowell, you are now under arrest by the order of the Assembly for the use of psychoactive magic on parties Conwyn and Hallowell. You will return to the Assembly for justice.*

What had the guys been doing while she'd spoken to me? They must have been frozen by magic too. Or... the enforcers might have killed them. That was what at least one sect of the Assembly's Justice division had done to a witch and her unsparked lover, according to a secret report that Kyler, my computer whiz consort, had uncovered.

Panic washed icy cold through my veins for an instant before another scrap of memory surfaced in my head. Just as my mind had been fading out with a knock-out spell, one of the enforcers had asked, *Should we dispose of the others?*

And the leader had snapped, *Think! Our orders were clear—no irreparable harm to her. We don't know which of these are her consorts.*

I closed my eyes and dragged in a breath, as slowly as my shaky lungs would allow. I shouldn't need to move to feel the magical bonds between myself and my four consorts. If they were at all nearby...

Relief trickled through me as I touched one and then another of their presences. Kyler's bright and buoyant spirit was down the hall, maybe a couple rooms from me. Damon, fiercely defiant as ever, was just a little farther. Seth's unshakeable energy reached me from the floor below us, with the more languid impression of Jin's right next to him.

And Gabriel? We weren't magically bonded yet. He'd come back into my life later than the others, and we'd only just confirmed the strength of our feelings for each other. My brow knit as I concentrated on his essence: all that steady confident charm, the glint of his bright blue eyes, the smell of him like forest moss laced with something faintly sweet.

There. I felt him, like a distant shiver, beyond Damon in this row of rooms. Fainter than the others without the consort bond, but present. All five of them, the boys who'd been my dearest friends in childhood, who'd become so much more since I'd returned to my family home a few months ago, were here and still alive. The quiver of life that reached me gave me hope.

No irreparable harm. For whatever reason, the Assembly hadn't wanted to simply destroy me. Maybe because it would be harder to cover up my death than that of some low-standing witch living away from witching society on an isolated island?

They'd realized I must have taken a consort—or

consorts. But they hadn't known who, at least not then. How much had they already figured out? They'd clearly determined that I'd only formed that bond recently. If my connection to the guys was severed in any way, including death, this early in our consorting, it would wreck me, mentally and magically.

The bigger question was how they'd known about any of that in the first place. What had the lead enforcer said in her accusation? *Parties Conwyn and Hallowell.*

Hallowell would be my father. They couldn't know for sure that I'd orchestrated the spell that had made him attack his colleagues with a magic artefact—that spell should have disappeared as its effects wore off—but they must have guessed after getting to Derek. Derek Conwyn, my former fiancé, former consort-to-be. The guy who'd conspired with my stepmother, and through her my father, to trap me in a consorting ceremony that would have put him in control of my magic and made me a virtual slave.

It hadn't occurred to me that the Assembly's investigators might track Derek down. The spell I'd put on him to prevent him from sharing what he'd learned about me would still have been active. As soon as they'd detected it, they could have lifted it off him. And then he could have told them straight that he'd seen me casting magic, that I'd told him I'd taken at least two non-witching men as consorts.

Which had brought them straight back to me.

I lowered my head to my covered hands. For just a few hours, I'd thought I'd gotten everything in place. I'd thought the guys and I could live a somewhat normal life, free to be together, even if I had to keep my magic secret from the rest of witching society. Pretending my spark had died with my twenty-fifth birthday, unkindled by any witching man, wouldn't have mattered to me one bit if we could have had more time like that last afternoon. Our little interlude in the house Seth had fixed up for us to share.

Now I'd be lucky if any of us made it out of this alive. The Assembly, or whatever part of it had been involved in enslaving other young witches like me, might want me living now, but who knew how long that would last? Maybe the investigators just wanted to question me to find out what else I'd done before they snuffed out my spark and my life.

A jitter ran through my body, emanating from the impressions I had of the five guys around me in the building. I straightened up and narrowed all my attention onto that sensation. An uneasy prickling ran down my back.

They were being magically prodded. Kyler and Damon, right now. The investigators would come to talk to the others soon, though. And they obviously didn't care about any policies around magical coercion when it came to unsparked people.

My fingers twitched inside their imprisoning mitts, but I couldn't move them enough to cast a spell. I took another deep breath and focused even more intently on those glints of life I held so dear.

There was already a magical connection between four of them and me, and all kinds of emotion if not literal magic between me and the fifth. I shouldn't need much effort, much motion to send my magic to them as a little shield against the investigators' influence.

I rolled my shoulders and shifted my head from side to side. The magic condensed around the flare of the brilliantly lit spark in my chest. At my mental push, some of that energy streamed in little threads toward the guys, latching on to them and filling them with a protective glow. It flowed quickly and smoothly to the four who were my consorts, through that tight bond between us. For Gabriel, I tipped my head again, a little extra push, a little extra energy. Maybe not as great an effect, but as much as I could give him.

No one was hurting my guys—not on my watch.

Philomena blinked into being on the bench beside me. Her appearing out of nowhere wasn't much of a surprise, because she was imaginary. I'd had few enough witching friends that I'd gotten in the habit of picturing the main character from my favorite historical romance as a conversational partner, and after several years she tended to pop up without even asking.

Now she looked as worried as I felt, her usually smooth forehead furrowed and her hands clenched in the folds of her immense skirts. "This is a nasty jar you've found yourself in," she said.

"Yeah, that's one way of putting it," I said. Phil knew all the best old-timey slang.

She peered at me, looking sad but fond at the same time. "It's not really me you need, is it, though?"

"What do you mean?"

"You have them." She nodded toward the door. "And

you've got your imagination. You can bring them to you just as easily as you brought me."

I could. Maybe the images I created wouldn't really be my guys, but I knew them well enough to know what they'd say, what they'd do, didn't I? Maybe having them here even that way would help center me so I could figure out what to do next.

Philomena waved goodbye and winked out of sight. I summoned up my guys in the room around me. They appeared as abruptly as Philomena had, exactly where it made the most sense for them to be. Seth sitting beside me, his strong arm hooked around mine. Jin at my other side, tracing patterns as if with paint on the back of my wrist. Damon stalking back and forth in the middle of the room, his dark blue eyes at full glower. Kyler bending over by the door to study the locking mechanism.

And Gabriel in the midst of them all, standing still and calm, his gaze fixed on me.

"What are we going to do about this mess, Sprout?" he said.

The childhood nickname brought a lump to my throat. Snuff my spark, I wished he and the rest of them really were here, not trapped apart from me in this prison.

"I don't know," I said. "But I'm going to figure out something. I got you all into it, so I have to get you out."

"We're standing by you because we wanted to," Seth reminded me, his arm tightening around mine. "And there's nowhere we'd rather be."

"Actually, I can think of a whole lot of other places I'd like to be," Damon muttered. He swiped a hand through his spiky hair and shot a softer glance my way. "But I don't blame you for a second, angel. It's these bastards who've been trying to control your life this whole time."

Jin leaned in to kiss my cheek, his familiar tangy smoky scent drifting over me. "We've worked our way out of a lot of jams before this. And whatever happens, it's been a wild ride. You know I wouldn't have missed it for anything."

Kyler shook his head, sending his tawny curls into disarray. "I can't hack my way through this—yet. You'd better believe I'm working on it."

He probably was, as well as he could, in his own cell. "I'm doing my best not to let them hurt you," I said. "I'll send all the magic I can. I—"

The voice in my head fell silent at the very real click of the lock disengaging. If I'd thought for even a second that my vision of Kyler had somehow managed to crack its code after all, that idea vanished along with the imagined guys a split-second later as the door swung open.

Three members of the Justice division walked in. The man who came to a stop directly in front of me I guessed was an investigator. The two women who flanked him wore the loose casual clothing of enforcers, designed to allow full freedom of movement if they needed to cast quickly. In other words, the exact opposite of my current bindings.

The woman at the investigator's left had a blunt bob of mouse-brown hair. She stared at me with a hard glint in her eyes, and I was abruptly sure she was the lead enforcer who'd taken me in. What did she have to look so pissed off about? I'd never done anything to her.

By all that was lit and warm, I'd never done anything to anyone who hadn't tried to do a hundred times worse to me first.

The jittering I'd sensed through my consort bonds shifted. I kept half my attention on the figures in front of me while adjusting the streams of my magic with an intake of breath. I couldn't let myself be distracted from the protection I needed to provide.

"Miss Hallowell," the investigator said. He didn't invite me to stand up to face him, just kept standing there looking down at me. I had the feeling he liked that position of superiority. "Do you understand why you're here?"

"I've been accused of unlawful magic," I said. "I wasn't given many of the details before your people carted me off here."

His lips curled into a smirk at my tart tone. "You'd already proven yourself quite resourceful and stealthy, Miss Hallowell. We needed to take appropriate precautions. The list of charges is rather extensive. Not just unlawful magic but also unlawful consorting. I'm sure you were not unaware of the expected proceedings when it comes to taking a consort."

"Self-defense," I said. "Does that count for anything? I found out my consort-to-be and my parents were planning to pervert the consort bond so that I'd be in pain if I didn't follow his commands. But I'm going to guess if you got assigned to my case, you already know about that and don't care."

His gaze didn't even flicker. Oh, he knew, all right.

He had to be part of the faction within the Assembly that had supported my father's actions, had apparently arranged for similar consortings for other young witches. The idea of it turned my stomach. Kyler and I had uncovered conversations between my father and a high-ranking Assembly member named Charles Frankford, but there was no telling how many of the people in the governing body over witching kind were part of that plot.

"So much for 'justice' then," I added. "Their unlawful magic doesn't count? You're supporting people who ignore their own sanctions. Who approved of witches being *enslaved*. I hope you're really proud of yourself."

I didn't know if going on the attack was the smartest move ever, but I obviously wasn't going to overcome these people with physical or magical force in my current condition. How much had the faction's lower members even thought about the schemes they were helping enact?

"We're going to focus on you for now," the investigator said smoothly. Okay, he didn't care what I thought of him. "To begin with, do you admit to using psychoactive magic on Derek Conwyn and your father?"

I couldn't see how admitting to any details directly was going to *help* me. Did he really think it was going to be that easy? I sat in silence, staring back at him.

He folded his arms over his narrow chest. "Have you magically compelled anyone else, witching or otherwise?"

My lips didn't budge. His eyes narrowed. Now I was getting a reaction.

"You understand that you can be compelled to give a response to these questions, do you not?" he said.

"Try me," I said.

He gestured to the mousy-haired enforcer. I braced myself with a twist of my body on the bench. A fresh flare of my magic shot up through my body to shield my mind the same way I was protecting my guys.

The enforcer stepped into a complex form, her arms and hands swiveling so quickly I couldn't follow the gestures. An instant later, a prickling of magic spread across my forehead. It dispelled against the barrier I'd constructed.

I might not be able to cast anything outside my body, but I could still work the magic inside myself as well as through the connections already in place.

The enforcer frowned and moved to try her coercive spell again. The investigator held up his hand.

"No point in wearing yourself out. We have time. It won't be long before at least one of them breaks—or her magic depletes itself." He smiled thinly at me. "Until we see each other again."

He turned on his heel and stalked out of the room, the enforcers right behind him. I sagged against the wall as the door thudded shut. But my gut was tied in knots.

He was right. My magic would deplete itself without my actual consorts next to me to help stoke my spark. And when I was out of energy, we'd be completely vulnerable to anything the enforcers threw at us.

CHAPTER TWO

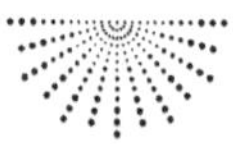

Gabriel

I almost would've been insulted that Rose's "Assembly" had sent just one person to deal with me—and that the person in question was a woman so short and skinny you could have taken her for a fifth grader if it wasn't for the lines starting to form at the corners of her eyes. Except I'd been around Rose and her witching kind for long enough to know that they didn't need physical strength to be plenty threatening.

This witch made that very clear from the moment she sat down across from me, with a quick flip of her hand. All at once, a piercing sensation formed at the back of my skull. My tongue seemed to loosen. I gripped the edge of the bench so tightly the hard underside dug into my fingers, but I could tell I wouldn't be able to withstand her magic.

I gritted my teeth, prepared to hold out as long as I

possibly could, and a whisper of Rose's energy washed over me. I'd have recognized her anywhere—even across a building, apparently. Her touch wrapped around my mind and deflected some of the pressure.

Only some. I couldn't imagine how many battles she might be fighting at the same time, between protecting herself and whatever she needed to do for the other guys. I couldn't ask for more help than she was already giving me.

That was okay. Self-control was a skill I had a lot of practice with. And I had my own ways of bolstering my resolve. I drew up my memories of Rose from the last few weeks like a shield. Rose's smile and embrace when I'd turned up at Jin's art gallery and found her waiting for me. Rose leaning into me as she admitted her fears. Rose's mouth against mine, her body hot beneath me. The rush of awe that shot through me when I watched her work her magic.

And love. That intensely tender swelling of love that awoke behind my ribs every time I thought of her.

I wasn't naïve to think that love could shield me from everything. But it made me even more ready to fight for it, for her.

The witch interrogator leaned forward in her chair, her eyes intent. She tapped her foot against the floor in an erratic rhythm that might have been strategic or just a personal tic. No other sound except that occasional patter penetrated the white walls of the little room they'd stuck me in. They had the air conditioning turned up too high. Goosebumps had popped up down my arms below the sleeves of my T-shirt.

"There's no point in fighting," the interrogator said. "We know at least some of you have completed the consorting ceremony with Miss Hallowell. Let me know whether you're one of her consorts, and we'll be done here."

I didn't believe that we'd really be done, not for a second. And especially not when she followed up the question with a flick of her fingers that sent another jolt of pain through my head. I winced in the second before Rose's moderating influence closed around it, numbing the worst of the effect.

These weren't the sort of people who simply had a little chat with you and then sent you on your way. No, they'd much more likely dump me lifeless in a ditch once they'd gotten what they wanted. They *had* done that to at least one other guy who'd hooked up with a witch, from the stories our brainiac Kyler had discovered.

"I don't think that's any of your business," I said.

She let out a huff of breath. "What has Miss Hallowell told you about witching society?"

"None of your business."

"Which of your friends has taken the role of consort?"

"None of your—"

Another spear of pain cut off my words and my breath. My tongue slipped. "They all—"

The pain numbed just slightly. I clamped my mouth shut, watching the interrogator. She was frowning, so I guessed those two words hadn't given her enough to draw any conclusions.

As she kept asking her questions, I kept repeating my

standard line. "None of your business." She asked about my job on Rose's estate and how I'd known her and what my association with the other guys was, but mostly she kept coming back to the same subject: Who Rose's consorts were. Whether I was one of them.

Apparently they couldn't just tell. I kind of liked the idea that a bond like that was private between the ones who'd formed it, unless they chose to tell people about it. Even if I wasn't one of the recipients of that bond. Yet. Possibly ever, if we didn't make it out of here.

I gathered myself, trying to find more of my own inner calm to steady myself alongside what Rose was offering me. An echo of her voice, just a couple nights ago, swam up in my mind. *Haven't you always done everything you could to help me, to help everyone you care about? I want all of you, even the parts you're scared of.*

There were ways I could work this. Turn the conversation around. Find a point of entry. I knew how to talk to people. Maybe that could get me somewhere useful.

"It's really important to you to put names on Rose's consorts, huh?" I said. "Just for your records?"

"Something like that," the interrogator said narrowly. Her shoulders had stiffened a little. She didn't like me asking *her* questions.

"Does that have anything to do with our arrest?" I asked. "Can a consort be charged for the same crimes as a witch because he helped kindle her magic?"

"You don't need to worry about facing those sorts of sanctions." Her tone was not at all reassuring. "It will simply help us get a full picture of the situation."

There was obviously more to it than that. What had Rose told us about consorting? Having an intimate partner was necessary for witches to maintain their magic, but if that was all these people were worried about, they could have killed us right now and cut her off permanently. What would it matter who was who? I didn't for a second believe they cared about sparing any of us who weren't that closely tied to her. We all knew too much.

But they didn't want to hurt Rose. The woman who'd led the charge when we'd all been taken had mentioned that. Was that it? Rose had also said the consort bonds could be broken, but not during the first few years when they were fresh—not without major consequences. She'd only taken the other guys as consorts in the last month. How much would it hurt her if those bonds were severed now?

A cold prickle ran down my back. That was it, wasn't it? They were trying to figure out which of us they could dispose of now without doing any damage to her.

The second they figured out I wasn't magically tied to Rose's well-being, it'd be dead in a ditch for me, absolutely.

"I think I get it," I said, testing out the idea. "You're worried about Rose—worried about how she might be affected by us if you shattered those consort bonds. That's it, isn't it?

The interrogator's lips pressed flat. That looked like a confirmation to me.

"I've told you, you don't need to worry about anything happening to you," she said.

My arm twitched with the urge to rub the back of my neck. The shackle around it held it to the bench. The spell she was aiming at me jabbed down my spine.

"Other than the magical brain attack you've got going on?" I said. Nothing would happen to me except a little tormenting.

She shrugged. "It's important we get this information quickly. That will be over when you're willing to talk."

How generous of them. I managed not to grimace. "*She* must be very important to you. But not because you're trying to make her happy, because this definitely isn't the way you'd accomplish that. So I'm guessing there's something you want to use her for."

The creases at the corners of the interrogator's lips deepened. Oh, yeah, they had a plan for Rose. Well, they could forget about getting anything from me they could put toward that.

"Miss Hallowell is guilty of several crimes," the woman said. "That is our only concern."

"Well, I can talk to you about that," I said easily. "I saw some of what was going on in her home. She was trying to protect herself exactly the way you would if someone wanted to sell you into slavery, I'd guess. Maybe you can tell me a little more about witching society. Do you have a concept of self-defense?"

"I think these matters are too complicated for you to understand," the interrogator said. "You need to start answering questions, not asking them. *Are you Miss Hallowell's consort?*"

With the emphasis she put on that last question, she seemed to scrap magical claws right across my brain. A shudder of agony ran through my body. My jaw jerked against my hold and dropped open. "None— None of— I—"

The cool balm of Rose's energy whispered over me again. I snapped my mouth shut in relief. The pain still radiated through my skull, but more like a bad headache than full-out torture.

Until the interrogator decided to up the ante even more. How long could Rose keep up this protection?

The woman inhaled as if she were about to ask another question, and the door to the room eased open. A young man poked his head around it.

"We're leaving them for now," he said.

The interrogator stood up. "What? I just need more time."

The guy shook his head and cut a glance toward me that looked eerily amused. "Give them time to think about their situation. And time for her to wear out her magic. Then it'll be easy."

If Rose ran out of magic—yeah, it probably would be easy. It had to be hard enough for her trying to shield all of us as well as she could even now. I swallowed a trickle of nausea.

The interrogator clearly wasn't convinced. She set her hands on her hips with a swish of her ponytail and glared at me.

"Is that what you really want? For us to exhaust her? You could end all this right now. You have no idea what else the next enforcer who comes for you might do. At least I was willing to stick to talking."

"Yeah," I said. "I'm very worried. Shaking in my

shoes here." I stretched out my legs as far as the chains attached to them allowed and arched an eyebrow at her.

The guy at the door chuckled. "You wouldn't be saying that if you had any idea what you haven't seen yet. Maybe we'll take you right out to the Cliff. I bet that'd terrify the answers out of you."

The interrogator turned her glare on him with a hiss of annoyance. He flushed and ducked back out.

"The Cliff, huh?" I said to her. "That sounds intriguing. Sure, let's take a trip out there."

"Don't you worry about the Cliff," she snapped, with more force than really made sense to me. What the hell was this Cliff that Rose's witching people were talking about like it had a capital C? She'd never mentioned anything about a cliff that I'd heard.

The interrogator strode to the door, but she made one last jerk of her hand before she headed out. Not even asking a question to go with it. Just reminding me how much she could hurt me. A burning sensation sliced through the top of my head. I bit my tongue trying not to make a sound, but she smiled. She could tell she'd hit the mark.

The second the door shut behind her, I sagged back against the wall. My head continued to ache dully. I wet my lips.

I didn't know what the Cliff was or what else the witches might have in store, but I definitely wasn't going to last all that long without Rose's help. How long *could* she hold out?

She needed me. I hadn't betrayed her, but how was I actually going to help her and the rest of us?

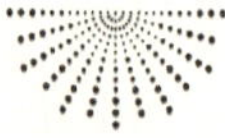

CHAPTER THREE

Rose

The magical pressure attacking Jin's mind eased off, and I tipped my head back against the wall of my cell. The hard surface behind me felt almost as distant as my impressions of my consorts.

It'd been hours of this—an attack on one guy and then another, sometimes two or three at once. Our bond made shielding all of them except Gabriel easy to an extent. But even doing something fairly easy wore a person out after a while. An ache ran from the top of my neck down my spine to my tailbone.

"They really could have stood to make this place more comfortable," Philomena remarked.

I didn't open my eyes. They felt too heavy. "It's a prison. They don't want me to be comfortable."

"I'm just making the observation. I truly feel they're doing a disservice to your high standing."

"I warped my dad's mind. I don't have any standing in witching society now. I'm lucky I'm even alive."

She sniffed, and her skirts rustled. "Not for very much longer, if this Assembly of yours has their way."

I shook my head. "They don't want to kill me. They'd have gotten it over with already if they did. There's something else they want from me." Maybe just a confession so they could lock me up without any repercussions from whichever Assembly members weren't aware of their conspiracy? Maybe more than that.

"Who gives a shit what they want?" Damon said.

My eyes popped open. Phil was still perched next to me on the bench, but my mind had brought my guys into being in imaginary form around me again too. Seeing them, knowing that their real selves were probably a lot more battered than they looked to me here, wasn't comforting anymore. The sight sent a sharper ache through my heart.

"When you know what people want, it's a lot easier to get people to do what *you* want," Gabriel said to Damon. He raked his fingers through his dark red hair, his gaze distant with thought.

"I don't think we're going to persuade these people of anything," Seth said from where he was standing by the door. "We've just got to get Rose out."

Jin traced a finger along the wall. "I wish it were as easy as drawing an exit on the wall and stepping through it." He cocked his head at me with his playful smile. "Or maybe it is, with your magic?"

"No," I said. "I don't know any spell like that—not

that I'm in much of a position to cast anyway." I lifted my bound hands.

"Your magic *is* probably our best chance of getting out," Kyler said, coming to stand by me. "How restricted are you with those restraints? You've been able to help us a little already."

"I can only do really basic things," I said. "Shift the magic through myself or connections already in place. To do anything larger or more finely tuned, I'd really need to use my arms and legs, my hands... It's the patterns and movements that direct the spell."

Gabriel's mouth slanted down. "And I guess it's a little much to hope you could break those restraints without using magic to do it."

"Yeah."

"Fuckers." Damon kicked the wall and spun around, tugging at his leather jacket. "We're not letting them get away with this."

My throat tightened. "I wish I could *really* talk to you. Find out what you've seen, what they've said to you." If I'd had the use of my full body, I might have been able to send thoughts back and forth with them... but I didn't.

I reached out to my sense of the actual guys again. The enforcers hadn't started up any new attacks since they'd left off Jin. Hard to believe they were actually giving me a chance to rest. But of course rest wouldn't replenish my magic. Only the loving touch of my consorts could do that, and my imagined versions of them couldn't produce the effect I needed.

Maybe they were giving me some time to think, to

realize how tired I was getting, before they came right at me again. I wasn't about to break yet—they couldn't know how brightly my spark had been lit with all four of my lovers—but by tomorrow? My heart sank at the thought.

And at some point I'd have to sleep. I wouldn't be able to keep protecting the guys if I wasn't conscious. I clenched my jaw against the urge to yawn.

"If we're going to do something, we need to do it soon," I said. "I just don't know what we can do."

"Oh, Rose." Philomena leaned against me, wrapping her hand around mine in its thick mitten encasing. Even through that, I felt a whisper of her touch. Because it was imagined, and no restraint could stop that.

All at once, my body went still except for the thud of my pulse.

Kyler looked up, his tawny curls jostling. "What is it, Rose? Did you think of something?"

"I might..." I tested the idea with my thoughts, having trouble believing I might actually have found the answer. But I couldn't think of any reason it definitely *wouldn't* work. "Dad always said I had a bit of an overactive imagination, and he didn't know the half of it. I've made Philomena practically come to life for years. I can see you here with me now as if you were completely real."

"You have an artist's mind," Jin said, still smiling. "Bringing what's in your mind into reality."

"That's exactly it." I sat up straighter. "The main part of a spell is mental—focusing on what you want. Figuring out the right words to call it up, where that applies. If I can *imagine* myself moving vividly enough... that might be enough to direct the magic even if I'm not physically in motion."

I had to try. Since I'd woken up here, it was the only option I'd thought of that had the slightest chance of working.

Phil clapped her hands. "Brilliant!"

I looked around at the guys. "I'm going to get you out of this prison if I possibly can. But I think for this I'm going to need every bit of my concentration. So I'll see you soon, for real."

They nodded and vanished. Philomena blinked out of the room too. I dragged in a breath, hoping my last words were true.

I might be able to cast a spell—so what spell was I going to cast? I had to get myself out of the room and free the guys from their cells, and then we'd need to escape this building and any protections around it. The latter part was going to be the hardest. As long as there were witching enforcers on hand who could throw their own spells at us, I couldn't hope we'd make it to the front doors.

Closing my eyes, I reached out with my mind again. Beyond my consorts and the fainter glimmer of Gabriel's energy, I could pick out the shivers of life of the enforcers and investigators in the building and around it. Here... and here... and over there... I pictured each shiver like a glint in the space around me.

A dozen or so here right now. If I could disable all of them at once, temporarily... A spell like the enforcers had cast on us, to knock us out before they brought us here. I could construct something like that, couldn't I?

I had to do it fast, before they figured out what I was doing and charged in to stop me. If I could even do it at all in this imaginary way.

I sucked in another breath and willed my thoughts quiet, my body still. Every shred of focus and energy had to go into this spell.

In my mind's eye, I saw the bindings on my hands, wrists, and ankles fall away. I stood up, careful not to tug on the chains and dispel the illusion. Behind my closed eyelids, I pictured my arms swaying, my legs sweeping in the beginning of a form. For a second, it felt so real a tingling raced through my nerves. My spark leapt with a burst of supernatural flame.

Yes. I could do this. Giddy with the exhilaration, I concentrated on the fine twists and dips of my fingers, gathering more and more magic into the spell, sculpting it into the shape I needed. My spark flared hotter. The magic seared through my entire body, quivering with the need to release.

Just a little more. Just a little sharper.

The little glints of the enforcers in the building twitched. A few of them were coming my way. My pulse skipped a beat. My hold on my imagined limbs wavered.

I had to do it now, before I lost my chance. Squeezing my eyes even more tightly closed, I pictured my arms whirling around me to spin the magic into a whirlwind. The energy rippled through me, stealing my breath.

Then with a real jerk of my waist, I sent it crashing out through the walls toward our captors.

The impact echoed through me: bodies falling to the floor, mental lights dimming. I gasped and focused another pulse of magic at my chains. With a wrenching I felt right through my chest, I shattered them. The mitts covering my hands burst in a spray of foam.

I scrambled to the door with real limbs that worked now. My legs wobbled under me. The spell had worked, but my whole body was aching from the effort, both of the amount of power I'd expended and the strain of doing it so completely mentally. My spark flickered, low and guttering, in my chest.

My magic was almost completely depleted. And I had no idea how long the enforcers would stay unconscious.

I stumbled and fell to my knees. No, I had to keep moving. With a shove against the floor, I propelled myself the last step to the door. My hand fell against the wall by the lock panel.

Just a little more magic. Please, by the Spark, let me have enough to finish what I'd started. At least now I could put my whole body to the task.

I murmured under my breath and jerked my fingers. Pain splintered down my arms—and the lock rasped over. I grabbed the handle and yanked.

The door swung open. I heaved myself out into the hall, my legs still swaying under me, my mind centered around one clear thought.

My guys. I had to find my guys.

CHAPTER FOUR

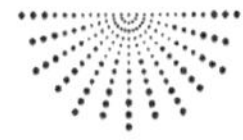

Rose

The long hall was all gray, the only color a red light on the lock controls next to the many doors. A body was sprawled on the floor at the far end: an enforcer, from her clothes. Maybe one who'd been rushing over to see what I was up to when my spell had hit them.

I had to keep moving, had to get all of us out of here before she and the others came to.

I staggered on past the first couple doors to the one where I'd sensed Kyler. My shoes scraped the floor, loud in the silence of the building. My hand trailed along the wall, feeling every tiny dimple in its mostly smooth surface.

One more step. Then another. There. My head was starting to spin, but I set my hands over the lock panel and made a quick twisting gesture, wrenching another flicker of energy from my spark.

The red light blinked green. The lock disengaged. I grasped the handle and hauled the door open.

The effort made me stumble halfway over the threshold. "Rose!" Kyler said, leaping to his feet. He'd been sitting on a bench like the one in my cell, his arms and legs chained like mine had been. The chains clinked as he tried to rush to my side and drew up short at their limit.

"I can get rid of those," I mumbled. "I can do it. Just let me..."

"Take it easy," he said as I made my dizzy shuffling way to him. "If you push yourself too hard—"

"If I don't push myself, we won't get out of here in time." I swiped my hands through the air, and links in his chains parted. The shackles were still attached to Kyler's wrists and ankles, but he didn't give me the chance to try to remove those too. He caught me in his arms, hugging me to him.

"Rose," he murmured into my hair. I'd never heard my cheerful computer enthusiast sounding so choked up. I hugged him back for a second, feeling a little relief just at the contact, the feel of his tall lean body against mine. Even after our imprisonment, his usual faintly minty smell still clung to his skin. I breathed it in, and my spark glinted brighter.

"We've got to go—find the others, get out of here," I said. "I knocked out everyone else in the building, but I'm not sure how long the spell will last."

"Right. Right." Ky grasped my hand, holding me

steady as we hurried out into the hall. "Do you know where the other guys are?"

"Damon's right here," I said, motioning to the door next to Ky's, from which an unmistakable prickly energy was emanating. "And Gabriel's on the other side of the hall two more down. Seth and Jin are down one floor."

Kyler's eyes widened at the sight of the enforcer on the floor. "Let me check her," he said, squeezing my hand and then letting go. "If she's got something to open the doors, you won't need to use up more of your energy."

He loped down the hall to where the enforcer was sprawled, and I turned to Damon's cell door. I couldn't afford to wait. Gritting my teeth, I motioned with my hands over the lock panel again. A thorn of pain jabbed my chest, but the lock slid over. I pulled that door open just as Ky let out a cry of triumph.

In his cell, Damon was pacing restlessly as far as his chains would let him, much like I'd imagined him. He jerked to a stop at the sight of me. "Rose! You got the bastards. Good."

"I'm getting you all out," I said. I tried to keep my steps steady, but I swayed a little on my way to him. He cupped his hands around my face as I worked my magic on his chains.

"You really are our angel," he said gruffly.

He kissed me, hard but quickly enough that I didn't protest. My fingers curled into his cotton tee. No leather jacket on the real him—it'd been too warm for that, the morning when we'd been arrested—but a lingering waft of that scent carried from his shirt. Then he was slinging his arm around my waist, supporting a little of my weight as we went to rejoin Kyler.

The slimmer twin was just stepping out of the cell he'd opened. He waved a keycard at us. "I can handle the doors now, but the chains are another story. No key that I could find."

"I can manage the chains," I said.

Gabriel was already standing, waiting, when I made my way in. Damon stayed next to me, his hand on my elbow. A wobble passed through my bones as I cast the spell to break the chains. Gabriel touched my cheek and kissed my forehead, and I fought the urge to sag into his embrace and just not get up for at least a year.

"You did it, Sprout," he said. "You're fucking amazing, you know that?"

"I haven't done it yet," I muttered, but I soaked up the warmth of his words all the same. "We've still got two more to go."

As much as I reveled in feeling them close to me, I hated that I had to lean on the guys—almost literally—the rest of the way along the hall and down the stairwell. Despite the brief kisses, my chest was aching around my spark again. My thoughts scattered and collected and scattered again.

I'd never worn myself out this badly before. I'd barely had the chance, since I'd only had my spark fully lit a short while ago.

"That door," I told Kyler, pointing. "And that one." He unlocked them with a swipe of the key card, which gave off a crinkling of magic as well. They had a spell on them that worked with the lock, I guessed.

Gabriel opened the door to Jin's cell, and Damon helped me in.

"We're making our grand escape?" Jin said as I split open his chains. "I wish I could have seen how you took them on."

"I just hit them with a spell to leave them unconscious for a while," I said. "I don't think it looked all that spectacular."

"Hmm. Briar Rose putting everyone else to sleep now." He stepped closer, and Damon shifted to the side to let my artist consort take his place. Jin hugged me and gave me a short but tender kiss.

In the last cell, Seth spread his wrists as far as they would go to give me a clear view of the chain between them. I broke it in an instant—and an instant after that, stumbled forward into him. He caught me against his tall brawny frame.

"Are you okay?" He glanced up at the others. "Is she hurt?"

"Just tired," I mumbled.

"She's been protecting us this whole time," Gabriel said. "And then knocking out the whole building—she must be exhausted. Come on. Let's get her out of here."

Seth scooped me up, cradling me against his shoulder. I made a murmur of protest, but really I wasn't in much condition to argue. *I* was starting to feel kind of numb, with an unpleasantly biting tingly sensation that was spreading from my ribs out to my limbs. Seth exchanged a glance with Ky, who nodded with a small smile to his burlier twin.

"All right," Gabriel said, falling into his usual role as

leader. "We need to find an exit, and we need some kind of transportation, because I don't think we're making it very far on foot."

"No kidding," Damon said in a snarky tone, but he craned his neck at the same time. "I think I see a bigger set of doors down at that end of the hall. Maybe that exit leads to a lobby?"

"If we're in Seattle in the main Assembly building—or near it—there's probably an underground parking lot," Ky put in.

"I haven't seen any elevators," Gabriel said. "Let's take a look around as quickly as we can."

Seth carried me along with the others with powerful strides. I nestled my head against his broad neck, absorbing his warmth and the sun-drenched bronze smell of him, but I kept my eyes open. I still had a little power left, if we needed one last burst of magic.

The double doors Damon had spotted led into another shorter hall. The door at the end required Ky's keycard. He peeked out and shut it again.

"It looks like a lobby. I can see traffic going by outside. We're definitely in a city. Do you think we're clear to just walk out, or could there be more of those Assembly people around, Rose?"

I frowned. "I'm not sure. I don't think they had time to warn anyone that I was trying something... But there could be a guard or two nearby that I missed with my spell. We'll be pretty noticeable going out there like this."

"There's a stairwell here," Jin said, opening a side door. "Stairs going down. Your underground parking?"

"We'd better take a look," Gabriel said.

We hustled down the stairs into a dimmer, cooler space with only a few vehicles parked under a concrete ceiling: a couple of sedans and a white delivery van. Gabriel made straight for the van.

"This will hold all of us—and be better for hiding us." He stopped and looked to me. "Can you manage this last door, Rose?"

I nodded against Seth's shoulder. When I shifted, he eased me down. I narrowed my eyes at the driver's side door on the van and sent a swift burst of magic at it.

The lock clicked over. Gabriel scrambled in and bent beside the steering wheel. "I should be able to manage the wiring. The rest of you get in, wherever you can."

I shouldn't have been surprised he knew how to hotwire a car, even though I'd have expected that more from Damon with his recent criminal associations. Gabriel knew cars inside and out, thanks to his dad who'd been the garage manager on my estate since before Gabriel or I was born. Until my dad had fired him because of Gabriel's friendship with me, that was. I didn't want to think about everything that had happened after.

But I did have to think about Gabriel. My heart wrenched, but I forced myself to touch his arm. "You don't have to stay with us, you know. We're not consorted. If you're not with me, they might leave you alone. They'll be so busy coming after the rest of us—"

Gabriel jerked around, setting his hand over mine. His bright blue eyes held my gaze intently.

"I'm not going anywhere, Rose. Not now, not ever. You don't have to offer. I knew what I was getting into already."

I swallowed thickly, but I couldn't help smiling. It wasn't as if I'd *wanted* him to leave.

"I lifted a phone off one of the guards," Kyler said, jogging around to the passenger side of the cab. "Already disabled anything that would let them track it. I can navigate. Is there anywhere you think we should go, Rose?"

I rubbed my forehead as if that would put my thoughts in better order. "We just need to get as far away from here as we can as quickly as we can, before anyone realizes and sounds the alarm. Someplace where we can get another car, I guess, since they'll start looking for this one."

"That's the start of a plan," Seth said. "Come on, let's get you in and resting."

Damon had already tugged open the van's back doors. We clambered in, Seth giving me an extra boost. A few boxes were stacked against one wall along with a dolly and a couple of thick wool blankets, I guessed for extra padding.

Jin grabbed the blankets and spread them on the floor. I sat down on one with a sigh of gratitude. Up front, the engine hitched and rumbled. Kyler let out a little cheer.

"Ready to go?" Gabriel called back to us.

"Almost!" Seth yanked the doors shut. He, Damon, and Jin gathered around me on the blanket. "Good to go!" he shouted to Gabriel, and then ran his hand over my hair. "Lie down. Get some rest. We can take care of you for a little while, all right?"

"If you need magic for anything, don't hesitate—wake me up," I said, and he nodded.

"Go to sleep, angel," Damon said, tugging me down next to him. I closed my eyes. The van rocked as it backed out of the parking space. My body was still aching, but with Damon holding me, Jin tracing gentle patterns on my back, and Seth stroking my knee, I didn't care.

I was with my consorts again. I'd saved them, at least for the moment.

Now we just had to find out whether we'd actually escaped or if we had another battle ahead.

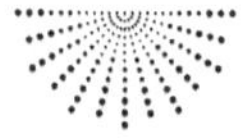

CHAPTER FIVE

Seth

We'd been on the road about twenty minutes when Kyler popped open the door between the seats up front and the van's storage area. "Hey, Damon," Gabriel called back from beside my brother. "Have you got any ideas about where we could find another van or a truck no one will be able to trace easily—and that won't cost a ton?"

"And why exactly are you asking me?" Damon muttered, but he got up to consult with them anyway. It wasn't exactly a secret that he'd been hanging out with some pretty questionable characters over the last several years. If any of us was going to know where to get something under the table, it'd be him.

"We'll want to pick up some burner phones too," Ky said. "I've got to tell my clients something, and Seth and I should probably send some kind of message to our parents, so no one worries when we don't show up for work."

Damon sighed. "I'm sure we can manage that too. Burner phones are pretty simple."

I shifted to take his former place beside Rose. She stirred and scooted closer to me, nuzzling my chest in her sleep. On her other side, Jin smiled at her with so much affection his face almost glowed in the thin light seeping through the back windows. He kissed her shoulder lightly and got up to check the boxes stacked by the van's wall. "I wonder if any of these have food in them. I'm starving. Aren't the rest of you?"

"We can look for somewhere to grab a meal after we've ditched this van," I said. "Rose said we should focus on getting as far away from the Assembly as possible until then."

"Oh, I know. But it can't hurt to check what we have."

As he shuffled through the boxes' contents, I lay my head down next to Rose's. Her scattered black hair still held a little of her usual light lilac scent. I'd just closed my eyes in the hopes of getting a little rest myself, my hand on her waist, when she gave a wordless murmur and stretched her arms. When I looked at her, her eyelids had fluttered open.

"I don't think you've gotten nearly enough sleep to recover from all that," I said.

"What about you?" she said, her dark green eyes still dreamy. "How much have you recovered?"

"I'm just fine," I told her. "But I didn't spend the last twelve hours shielding five other people and myself."

She wrinkled her nose at me. Then her expression turned serious. She touched the side of my face. "Did I manage to shield you? They didn't hurt you?"

"Not really," I said. "I felt you there—I felt your magic inside me. Theirs wasn't strong enough to get past it."

"Good."

"But I could see how much that took out of you. So more rest. That's an order."

"You're a renovator, not a doctor," she protested. A sly smile crossed her face. "Besides, maybe it's not sleep I really need to recover."

I was tired too, but somehow that one look from her sent a bolt of desire right from my chest to my groin. I raised an eyebrow at her. "Is that an invitation?"

She shrugged, still grinning. "If you want to take it as one."

Oh, I did. And I knew she was more drained of magic than anything else after everything she'd done to protect us and get us out of that prison. Helping her replenish that energy came with the extra bonus of getting to enjoy *her* in one of my favorite ways.

I traced my fingers across her cheek and into her hair, tugging her into a kiss. She kissed me back hungrily but not forcefully. Her hands balled against my chest. I had the sudden feeling that she was holding herself back, holding her needs in check—worried about me. My heart swelled with a wave of love.

I eased back half an inch, just enough to speak while our breaths mingled. "Hey. You take everything you need. I want this. I always want this."

"Seth..." She drew in her breath as if to say something more, and then the van rocked with a dip in the road. It tipped her toward me, and I let our mouths collide again.

Rose relaxed against me with a pleased sound in her throat. She kissed me back harder, her hands slipping up to run over my short-cropped hair and then down the front of my chest all the way to the fly of my jeans. My cock sprang to attention.

But we didn't need to take this interlude quite that fast. If she needed the energy our coming together could give her, then I wanted to stretch that coming together out for as long as I could, and to bring her every imaginable pleasure along the way.

I teased my fingers down the side of her neck as we kissed again. They stroked over the curve of her breast, bringing her nipple to a point through her bra. Rose hummed encouragingly and pressed closer. Her hand slid up under my shirt, drawing sparks over my skin.

I'd almost forgotten Jin was in the back of the van with us until I heard his intake of breath. He knelt by Rose's back. "Speaking of hungry," he murmured, sounding amused.

Rose kissed me once more and turned her head toward him. As he leaned in to press his lips to hers, I eased down her body, tugging her shirt up and her bra aside. Jin's hand teased over her stomach, and my mouth closed over the tip of her breast. Rose whimpered and arched into me. She yanked more insistently on my jeans.

Oh, fuck. How could I deny her? My woman. My consort. My *Rose.*

I fumbled with the button, and she was tugging my

jeans down the second I released it. Jin eased his hands down her body to peel off her own jeans. Rose's fingers closed around my cock, and somehow it got even harder than it had already been.

"Rose," I said hoarsely, and maybe it wasn't just her who needed this. I hadn't been with her, been *inside* her, in days. Suddenly it felt like years.

My lips crashed into hers. She moaned into my mouth as Jin stroked her breasts, and her grip on my erection tightened. I groaned in return.

She wrenched my boxers down after my jeans. The naked head of my cock rubbed against the dampness on her panties. The floor of the van quivered beneath us, but in that moment it only added to the sense of urgency.

My mouth slipped down to taste the skin of her neck as my hand dipped beneath that last scrap of fabric. "Yes," she said breathlessly. The heel of my hand pressed against her clit. I dipped a finger right up inside the hot center of her, and she gasped.

Jin claimed her mouth again, still fondling her breasts. Rose reached behind her to tug at his pants too. He paused for a second, catching her eyes, and when she smiled, he unzipped them. As I added a second finger to pulse inside her, her other hand closed around Jin's freed cock. She pumped both of us at an accelerating rhythm. Then she hooked her leg over my thigh.

"I need more of you inside me, Seth," she said around a whimper. "I need to feel all of you."

I kissed her hard and pulled her panties aside at the same time. She guided my cock straight to her slick center. I let out another groan as her tight heat closed around me. It was bliss, just like always.

I set a steady rhythm of my own, plunging in and out of her in time with her panting breaths. Her fingernails dug into my shoulders. I kept my hand on her hips, helping keep us in sync as she bucked into me. Then my thumb slid lower, working over the little nub right above the place where our bodies joined.

Rose quivered, rocking faster. She caught my mouth with hers, and right then I could feel it: the crackle of energy we were generating together, her and me and Jin. It seared between us and sank into her skin.

Jin's breath stuttered. He pressed his mouth to Rose's shoulder as his hips jerked. I kept my own release under tight control. I could give Rose even more. Take her over the edge and then right back over it again, if I kept my self-control.

"Oh!" she cried out as I thrust into her deeper. My thumb swiveled over her clit, and she clenched around me, so tight my balls squeezed and I almost lost it.

Almost. I caught myself just in time, clenching my muscles against that release. Oh, God, it was hard not to let go while she shuddered against me. The heat I'd felt between us before flared even hotter.

Her rocking slowed. She looked at me through her eyelashes as I continued to thrust gently into her. The flush of her cheeks against her pale skin was so beautiful it sent an ache through my gut. "You didn't finish," she said softly. "More?"

"I want to give you everything I can," I said. "I want to take you even higher."

She let out a breath shaky with pleasure. "Mmm, yes." Then she lifted her head.

Jin had scooted back from us, cleaning up with a grin, and Damon had returned from his chat with the guys up front. He took in the scene we'd made, his eyes darkening with lust, but he stayed where he was. Until Rose raised her hand to him.

"Are you sure?" he said, his voice rough.

Her smile grew. "I get just as much from giving as from receiving."

He let out a chuckle. "Well, in that case, who the hell am I to argue?"

It was almost painful, sliding all the way out of Rose as she rolled over. But a second later she was urging me back into her from behind. I pushed into her sex with a groan, caressing her side, her breasts, her ass as I set a new rhythm. My fingers settled back over her clit.

Rose sighed in pleasure. Then she motioned Damon even closer, undoing his jeans. A wordless mutter escaped him as she slicked her tongue over his cock. "Oh, angel, there's no better heaven than this. I swear it."

I never would have thought, a couple months ago, that I'd have wanted to see a woman I loved getting it on with another guy—even if I was getting it on with her at the same time. But now, knowing the bond we all shared, knowing how much we all meant to her, it turned me on even more to feel all the pleasure humming through the room.

Pleasure and the sizzling energy that must be feeding her spark. As I thrust harder, fingering her at the same time, that energy seeped deeper into my own skin. Or maybe it was seeping out of me?

A clamping sensation formed around my ribs. Not exactly pleasant, but I could take it. I'd promised I'd give her everything. She'd already given everything for me and the other guys back at the prison.

I was the strongest one here. Better me than anyone else.

Rose's body started to quiver around me again. I flicked my fingers against her clit, soft and then hard and then soft again. She moaned around Damon's cock. His breaths were coming as harsh as mine now.

I kissed the back of Rose's shoulder, driving myself as deep inside her as I could, seeking that sensitive spot I knew could set her off. Bliss radiated through my body, melting the edge off the clamping sensation in my chest. Damon groaned and clutched Rose's hair, and Rose gave a shaky cry. As her sex contracted around me a second time I couldn't hold back any longer.

I spilled myself inside her with a rush of pleasure and relief. The pressure around my ribs eased off.

Rose tugged Damon all the way down onto the floor and pulled us both up against her, snuggling between us. I hugged her waist, content just for a moment to lie there in the hazy afterglow. Trying not to think about what she might need all this magic for that still lay ahead of us, and how much she might have to expend all over again to protect us if her Assembly caught us now.

A minute later, the van jerked to a stop. "All right, love birds," Kyler called cheerfully from up front. "Make yourselves presentable. It's time to ditch this van."

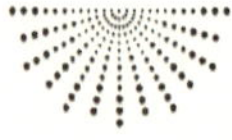

CHAPTER SIX

Rose

I woke up at a bump of the tires. Thin dawn light and a stretch of pine trees welcomed me from outside the window of the seven-seater SUV we'd commandeered last night. I lifted my head from the cheap jacket I'd bought during the same quick stop, which I'd been using for a pillow. My neck throbbed from the awkward position it'd been bent in. With a flick of my fingers, I sent a soothingly cool waft of magic through the muscles there.

Over the tops of the seats ahead of me, Seth's tawny hair showed where he sat at the wheel. Jin had taken over navigating beside him while Kyler slept in the middle seat next to Damon. Gabriel had his head leaned against the window across from me in the back seat, but he straightened up when he noticed I was awake.

"Where are we?" I asked. I'd drifted off not that long

after we'd found the car and a hasty meal at a fast food drive through, with instructions that the guys had to wake me up right away if they saw any trouble. They hadn't woken me, which had better mean trouble had stayed away so far.

"Somewhere around the middle of Montana," Gabriel said. "Ky figured that was the most isolated route."

"And I was right," Ky piped up from the seat in front of us, where I guessed he wasn't sleeping anymore. "We haven't seen anything but trees in at least an hour." He paused. "Where do you think we go from here, Rose?"

I didn't know. That fact made my stomach ball into one giant knot. All I'd been able to think about before was getting us away from that corrupt faction of the Assembly and the enforcers they'd commandeered to their cause. But I'd gotten the guys into this mess, so now I had to find a way through it.

"We can't go back to the Hallowell estate," I said. "Obviously. But I guess... Back before this all blew up, I thought maybe we could run away somewhere. Find a place where nobody would know who I was and just live our lives there. We could still do that. We'd have to be more careful, since obviously the Assembly would be keeping an eye out for us now... But there aren't that many witches in the world they could have on the look-out for us. It wouldn't be that hard to keep a low profile. If we're not hurting anyone, eventually they'll have bigger problems to focus on."

"Finding a place to just live our lives doesn't sound so

bad," Gabriel said, setting his hand on my knee with a reassuring squeeze.

Maybe not to him. He'd spent the last few years rambling all over this continent and South America too. He'd lost his dad to a suicide that was partly *my* dad's fault, and he'd told me his mom and her new family had turned him away. I wasn't sure he had anyone, really, except for us.

But the other guys did.

"It's not really fair to all of you, though," I said. "None of you would be able to reach out to your parents or your friends or anyone you know back home, because you can be sure the Assembly would be keeping an eye on them now that they know who you are. Even sending any more messages from a new phone would be risky. You shouldn't have to give up every bit of contact with those people."

Damon shifted in his seat. "What's the alternative?" he said. "Let the bastards hunt us down? I'm sure we can find ways to at least let the people we care about know we're okay. To get a little money to my mom here and there. Your magic was strong enough to beat these assholes before."

Maybe I could find a way to let them keep some contact with home without putting us in danger. It was hard to think that far ahead. I rubbed my forehead.

"For now, let's just find a good spot to hide out, and then we can make longer term plans from there," Jin said, turning to look back at us. He smiled at me. "One thing at a time."

"Yeah," I said, but the knot in my stomach didn't relax.

What could I have done differently in those months since I'd arrived back home and fallen back in love with the guys who'd always been there for me? I couldn't really say. Pretty much any other option I could think of would have ended up with me enslaved, in agony if I didn't perform magic to Dad or his chosen consort's orders, or one or more of us dead. My stepmother *was* dead, I had to assume because Dad and his associates hadn't wanted to risk her revealing her part in the plan.

That meant there had to be a significant portion of the witching community who wasn't part of that conspiracy, didn't it? If they felt they needed to resort to murder to cover their tracks... they must be covering them from a lot of people.

I just didn't know who I could trust. I'd used to think I could trust my father. I'd used to think I could trust the entire Assembly. So much for that.

What did I know about the faction that had supported Dad's plan? It definitely included Charles Frankford, who was high up in the Assembly—head of the Education division. He was the one who'd been casually chatting with Dad about strategies for controlling my magic. There'd been those dozen or so people in the prison building, but I couldn't be sure even all of them were in on the plot. I didn't think more than five or six had been involved in the interrogations at any given time.

"When the investigators came to talk to you in your

cells," I said, "was it always the same people? Or did different ones come each time? What did they look like?"

"It was always the same woman with me," Gabriel said. "And one time a guy came to talk to her, but he never was part of the questioning. The woman was really small—short and thin—and maybe in her thirties? With a ponytail—blond. I think she was in the group that 'arrested' us."

"I only saw one woman, but not that one," Damon said. "The one who was badgering me had dark brown hair, shoulder-length I guess, and she was pretty tall. She was in that first bunch too."

Jin nodded. "I saw one woman and one guy. The same woman as Damon, it sounds like."

"And I saw the one with the ponytail Gabriel mentioned," Kyler said.

Seth pitched his voice back toward us, his gaze still on the road. "I saw the one with the blond ponytail a couple times, and another one with long black hair once."

And then there was the mousy-haired woman and her partner who'd stood by for my interrogation. So definitely at least five witches and a few male interrogators as well. I bit my lip. "And what did they ask you about? Did they say anything about what they wanted, what they were trying to do, that sounded useful?"

"Mostly they just asked about whether I was your consort and which of the other guys was too," Damon muttered. "I told them they were way too obsessed with other people's sex lives."

I bit back a laugh. "Yeah."

"I got the same line of questioning," Kyler said. "They didn't really talk about anything else. I don't think they figured *we* could tell them anything else useful."

The other guys were nodding. "It's because of the bond, right?" Gabriel said, watching me. "They didn't want to keep us around, but they were worried about how it'd affect you if they got rid of us."

Ah. I shouldn't be surprised that he'd figured that out. Maybe the other guys had too.

"Something like that," I said. "I mean, as well as I can guess. They didn't tell me what they wanted either. Other than I have to assume they wanted me alive at least for now." Or we'd all already be dead. "I have no idea what for."

"After what they've already tried to do to you, I think we can assume it's nothing good," Jin said.

"There was something else one of them mentioned to me." Gabriel frowned, his eyes going distant. "Something about a cliff? The way he said it, it sounded significant. Like that's the name of some special place: The Cliff."

"The Cliff," I repeated. "That doesn't ring any bells. But there's clearly a lot I didn't know about certain parts of witching society."

"That phone I lifted from the woman in the prison died," Kyler said, holding it up. "I didn't even think about buying a charger that'd work with it during our rush at that last stop. But as soon as we go through someplace I could buy one, I'll do some more digging on it and see what I can find. I might even be able to find a backdoor into their network."

Damon snorted. "If we ever see anything other than trees again."

"We could pass through a decent-sized town in about an hour," Jin said, consulting the paper map we'd bought. "If you think—"

His voice cut off with a hitch of breath. Beside me, Gabriel flinched. A wave of magic hummed through the air around us, thin but obviously potent enough to do some damage.

The enforcers. They'd latched onto us somehow, determined our location—or maybe it'd been a general sweep.

My arms had already started moving before I needed to think. I worked my hands through the protective motions I could now draw with full strength, unchained. A deflective hum of my own magical energy coursed through the bonds between me and my consorts and wrapped around Gabriel. The painful probing spell dissipated.

The rumble of the engine had softened. Seth pulled over to the side of the road. "I'm not sure it's safe to drive if they're going to hit us like that."

"I think it's over now," I said. "I pushed them back. They—"

It came again, a wave twice as forceful as before. Hard enough that my own ears rang with the impact. My hands whipped out, but Gabriel had already grunted in pain. Jin had stiffened in his seat. Fuck. No. I wasn't going to let them hurt my guys any more than they already had.

I wove the protective spell thicker, stronger, and cast

it out. Jin's shoulders sagged. Someone in the middle seat exhaled in relief. Gabriel swiped his hand past his temple as if he'd been left with a residual headache, but when I gave him a questioning look he just shook his head.

I kept moving my arms and weaving with my fingers, spinning a few more layers of the spell so it could settle in place over them. My skin prickled with the sense that another rush of magic had flung itself against my shield, but the guys didn't show any reaction other than a twitch of Gabriel's jaw, which might have been just about anything.

"You're all okay now?" I asked.

"If they're still throwing stuff at us, I don't feel anything," Damon said.

"All good here," Gabriel added.

"Okay." I took a deep breath. "I'll just have to keep working that magic as they wear it down—if they keep at us."

Seth glanced back at me, his expression even more solemn than usual. "What are the chances they won't?"

"Not very high," I had to admit. I brought my hands to my face. "I don't know how they even found us. There isn't any spell I know that should reach that far and that accurately across that much distance." Unless they'd done something to me or the guys back in the prison that I hadn't realized? I had no idea. This illicit faction of the Assembly might have all kinds of magical strategies they kept to themselves for their malicious purposes.

"I vote we don't hide out anywhere near here, anyway," Ky said, somehow managing to sound cheerful even now.

I couldn't stop a halting laugh from slipping out. "No, I guess not."

"So, what do we do now?" Seth asked.

"Whatever you need us to do, we're on it," Damon said. "Just say the word, angel. You know that."

I did. I pushed my hands back into my hair and then dropped them to my lap. What could they do? I didn't even know what *I* could do. But like Jin had said before, we had to start someplace. One step at a time.

"We keep going," I said. "Change up our route. Zigzag a little, maybe. Damon, any evasive techniques you've got, pass them on. And then..." I sucked my lower lip under my teeth. "If they're going to come at us with magic I've never seen, then I guess I'm just going to have to get creative right back at them."

CHAPTER SEVEN

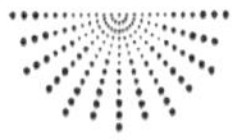

Jin

The town we'd stopped in was large enough to have a big box store on the outskirts where Kyler found his charger and we all got a couple fresh changes of clothes—but small enough that I got a few stares as I ambled through the grocery store. I'd bet they didn't see a whole lot of Korean guys with blue-streaked hair passing through here. I just smiled and grabbed the best non-perishables I could find to fuel our stomachs on this little road trip.

Maybe I'd open their minds a little. Or maybe they'd just mutter about that weirdo and his strange grocery shopping habits when I was gone. I was fine with it either way. I'd learned to let other people's opinions roll off my back a long time ago, growing up in our much smaller town back home.

The cashier seemed totally unfazed, even when I dug

out a wad of cash to pay for my stack of groceries. The Assembly people had confiscated our wallets, but Rose had done her magic on a bank machine a while back to get us into our accounts—and to increase our daily limits by a substantial amount. We'd taken out all the cash we had on hand, since we didn't want to leave an electronic trail any farther than that. For all we knew her witchy enemies could shut those accounts down now that they knew we were on the run.

Rose was waiting by the SUV when Seth and I hauled the bags of groceries back there. She took a couple from me to help us arrange them in the trunk. As soon as my hands were free, I had to restrain myself from pulling her to me and getting lost in a kiss, just for a minute or two. We were trying not to draw *too* much attention.

But it was hard not to want to touch her, to remind myself how real she was, when just yesterday I hadn't known for sure whether I'd lost her forever. Whether any of us would see each other again, or anyone else, for that matter.

We were all here—here with her—and every now and then when I remembered that little white room and the chains and the pain in my head, that fact felt like a miracle.

I settled for taking her hand. "Where did the other guys get to?"

"Gabriel's seeing if he can buy some extra gas so we can fill up on the road if we decide we don't want to risk even going into a station," she said. "Damon went with him to help carry. And Kyler spotted a pawn shop with some tech stuff in the window—he ducked in to take a quick look. They should be back in ten or so."

"Do you think the Assembly's 'enforcers' will be following us on the road as well as with their magic?" Seth asked.

"Probably," Rose said. "It'll be a lot harder for them to stop us from a distance. But I didn't get much sense of them through their magical attack, so I don't think they can be very close yet."

My gaze settled on a craft shop farther down the main street. My fingers itched with the familiar urge for a paintbrush or a lump of clay. The impulse brought to mind another use I'd made of my art.

"Hey," I said. "You said you were going to need to get creative to stop these assholes. Could we put together another merging of art and magic? You had me make that necklace to repel your fiancé. Would something like that work to hold off these attacks?"

Rose's eyes brightened. "It should. And it couldn't hurt to add a new strategy into the mix."

"Well, then, I'll be right back." I gave her a grin and a salute, and jogged over to the shop.

Ten minutes later I had myself some leather string, acrylic paint and brushes, and several wooden tokens that weren't exactly ideal pendants, but would have to do. I'd also grabbed a roll of canvas and a pack of small gesso-coated boards in case we could find some use for those too. When I got back to the car this time, the rest of the crew was already waiting.

"I guess you can't really paint while the car is on the move, right?" Rose said. "Too many vibrations?"

"Not ideal for fine detail work," I agreed.

"Let's get some more distance from the last place they were able to hit us and then find somewhere off the beaten track to stop for a little while," Gabriel said. "I'm sure we could all use some more rest when we can get it. We'll all think clearer that way too."

"Sounds good to me."

"I'll try to figure out where they are when they send more magic after us," Rose said. "As long as we stay far enough ahead of them, they can't hurt us that much anyway." But her face was drawn as she said it. I had the feeling she was more worried than she wanted to let on.

Well, why not? We'd done everything we could to keep our secret safe from her Assembly, and they'd found us out anyway. If we could actually have any kind of life now that wasn't constantly on the run, that *would* be a miracle.

But we'd have a better chance if I could help make it happen.

* * *

Not long after the country road we'd been driving down had shifted from pavement to bumpy gravel to bumpier dirt, Gabriel pulled the SUV over by a small clearing off to the side. The sun was heading back down the sky, a late afternoon stillness settling over the landscape. I sat up straighter where I'd been dozing in the middle seat. My mind immediately started drifting over the possibilities.

"This is the spot we're taking our break?"

"We're pretty far from any habitation," Rose said. "No one around to notice us. And the enforcers have let up on their attacks for a while. I think this is the best we're going to get." She glanced around the car from where she'd taken the front passenger seat to navigate. "Seth and Gabriel, I think you guys should get the first chance to really sleep. You two have done most of the driving so far."

Seth looked like he was going to argue, but she gave him a look so firm he shut his mouth. From the way he rubbed his eyes, he had to be feeling some fatigue. It wasn't like a big guy like him could get the best sleep sitting cramped in a car anyway.

"I'll take the back seat," Gabriel told him, clapping him on the arm as he clambered past. "You take the middle." With three seats, it was the longest section.

Kyler hopped out, his gaze glued to his stolen phone. "I'm making some progress with this. I'll keep at it for the time being."

Damon followed him. As his feet hit the ground, his head swiveled to take in our surroundings. "I'm going to keep watch," he said, nodding to a stand of trees near the side of the road where he'd be able to see down a long stretch of it. "Maybe they stopped using magic because they're trying to sneak up on us."

"Thank you," Rose said to him, giving him a quick kiss that left his eyes bright. Then she turned to me. "Time to get painting?"

I grabbed my bag of supplies and checked the clearing for a good spot to set up shop. There was a log lying beside a short row of trees at the opposite end. I walked over to it, my shoes rustling through the long grass. The sharp scent of the scattered dandelions reached my nose. They might be weeds, but I'd always loved the contrast of that stark yellow with the deeper green of their leaves.

Sitting on the log gave me a twinge low in my gut. It was on a different log that I'd first made love to Rose—in a headlong rush after the consort ceremony in the forest on her estate's grounds, when we'd all collided in a blaze of magic and passion. I suspected that now I wasn't ever going to be able to take a walk in the woods without getting a little bit turned on.

I handed a pencil and six of the wooden tokens I'd picked up to Rose. "Sketch the glyph you need me to work with. Will I need to hide the symbols in the rest of the image like before?"

"I guess not," she said. "Since anyone who comes after us will already know I'm doing magic. The spell might work even better if you emphasize the lines of the glyph. We'll just want to keep the pendants tucked under our shirts in case we cross paths with anyone else from witching society who wouldn't recognize us otherwise."

The tokens were about half the size of my palm, so that seemed doable. I nodded and started laying out my paints while she sketched.

"Maybe there are other ways we can combine art and magic," I said. "You've only just come into your powers, and you've had to keep them secret the whole time... You should experiment, stretch yourself, find out what you're capable of."

"Like you do with your art?" Rose said with a smile.

"Why not? Creating spells looks kind of like art to me. Like a dance—or a martial art."

"Okay, I can see what you mean with the forms." Her smile turned crooked. "I did experiment a little when we were in that prison. I managed to cast with barely any motion, just imagining the forms. But that took at least twice as long and three times as much energy as a proper magicking. It doesn't do me any good to burn myself out that fast unless it's that or not cast at all."

Her brow furrowed in concentration. She handed the first token to me. "You know what I'd really like? I'd like to make them all forget they ever knew me or the rest of you, or cared what happened to us, forever and ever. I think that might be a little beyond any one witch's powers though."

My heart squeezed at the longing in her voice. I'd only known the pressures and restrictions of the witching world for a couple of months and mostly just through her. She'd had to live with them hanging over her for her entire life. It was because of those pressures and restrictions that she'd been torn away from our friendship and her home in the first place.

I got to work painting the first token, letting the colors bring the lines of the glyph to brilliant life instead of obscuring them like I'd needed to before. Rose finished her sketching, set the rest of the tokens on the log between us, and stood up. She stepped tentatively into the deeper grass as if testing the ground. Then she really started to move.

It did look like a dance, the motions of her magic. I looked up to catch glimpses as I worked, and when I'd finished the first one I stopped for just a minute to take it in.

Her arms swept through the air, and her feet glided across the ground. Her whole body undulated with the power she could channel through it. My breath caught with awe, just watching, not even knowing what she was creating with that energy.

She stopped, her own breath coming a little short, just as I started on the fourth token. "You know, I think I did find something else I can use, exploring those feelings," she said. "I protected you all before using the consort bond, that magical connection we already have in place. I might be able to tie another spell to that and each glyph. Make it personal, and stronger that way—and let the energy of the bond enhance the spell. That way I wouldn't have to keep 'recharging' it with more power."

"That sounds brilliant," I said. "There you go. That's why I'm a firm believer in experimenting."

A short laugh spilled over her lips. She pushed back her dark hair, which was gleaming under the late afternoon sun. Then her smile faltered. "Except with Gabriel. Because we don't have that connection yet."

"You could try the consort ceremony with him."

She shook her head. "He only just started to feel comfortable opening up to me. I can't ask him to make a decision like that just to make things easier for me. I wish I hadn't needed to turn to the rest of you the way I did, and there was a lot less pressure on you then. At least, the way things are now, he'd still have a chance of going back to a normal life."

I raised my eyebrows at her. "Do you really think for one second he'd ever agree to that?"

"Well, maybe not. But who knows, if things get a lot worse... I just wouldn't feel right taking away that option. Asking him to do it. When we're safe, when things have settled down, then we can have that conversation."

"I hope you know that I've never regretted committing myself to you and the rest of this," I said as I set down the fourth token. "And I think I can say that none of your other consorts have either."

Her smile came back, soft but bright enough to light me up inside. "I know, Jin. And you can't imagine how amazed I am that I managed to get this lucky."

She bent to kiss me, and this time I could give in to that urge without any fear of spectators. I kissed her back with all the adoration I had in me until I knew I had to get back to the task at hand.

"Just two more," I said. "I think the first one, at least, is dry now. You could start adding the spells to them."

"Perfect." She picked that one up. "They're beautiful, as always."

"You inspire me," I said with a wink. But it wasn't just flirting. I meant it. I couldn't imagine what I might come up with if I had a chance to really settle back into my art now that she was in my life so fully.

I finished the last two tokens and then sat back to watch Rose do her casting. Somehow, I could tell that her movements now were more focused, with a clear purpose instead of tentative exploration of the possibilities. She was just dipping low over the fifth token, her hands swirling in the air, when a shock of a different sort of magic walloped me across the head.

Thanks to Rose's earlier protections, the impact only made me reel for a second, like a strong blast of wind had hit me. I hated to think what I'd have felt if she hadn't put a shield around me. Rose went still, standing over the token, her eyes widening. She murmured a few words and whipped around in a different, more frenetic casting.

"They're close now," she said, ducking to scoop up the tokens. "We don't have time to stay and do the rest. I think they've almost caught up with us."

Shit. I tossed my remaining supplies in the bag and ran with her back to the car.

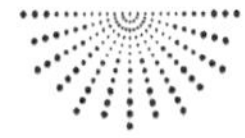

CHAPTER EIGHT

Rose

The SUV swayed as Damon took it around a sharp bend in the highway. I wasn't sure whether letting him drive had been a smart move or a stupid one, but he definitely knew how to speed.

"Well," Philomena said, appearing briefly beside me. "This is certainly exciting."

I rolled my eyes at her and then called to Damon from the back. "Hey! We left them behind hours ago. The last time they sent any magic our way, they were so far away I couldn't get a sense of them anymore. Fast is good, but let's not overdo it and end up in a ditch."

"I've never put a car in a ditch yet," Damon said. I could hear his smirk in his voice.

Phil fluttered her fan in front of her face. "I'm not sure I believe that." But she didn't look all that put out. She'd been involved in a carriage crash in the novel I'd imagined her out of—but it had ended with a rather passionate encounter that she hadn't minded at all.

"I think we should take a right up here," Jin said beside Damon, squinting at the map in the fading sunlight. Evening was turning into dusk outside. "Better to keep changing direction regularly so we're harder to track, right?"

"That's the theory," Ky said from the seat in front of me. The glow of the phone he'd grabbed hazed the area around him. Next to him, Seth had fallen back asleep with his head tipped against the window. He'd stayed reasonably alert for the first frantic race away from the clearing, but as the danger had appeared to retreat, exhaustion had caught up with him again. I wasn't sure he'd slept at all yesterday.

I swiveled my hand, sending a little more magic to the barrier around him. Since I'd only had time to finish the full spell on four of the pendants, I wasn't wearing one. Seth had insisted that he could go without until I had the time and space to finish the others. I wasn't going to let him regret that decision. He might have more muscles than the rest of us, but that hardly made him invulnerable, especially when it came to magic.

My reinforcing spell came not a moment too soon. Another jittering wave of probing, jabbing energy rushed over us. I made a quick gesture to deflect more of it from me, reaching out through it for any impression of our attackers at the same time. Philomena faded away as my concentration shifted. Then I noticed Gabriel's wince where he was sitting by the opposite window.

"Gabriel." I grasped his elbow. His painted glyph

hung beneath his shirt from the leather string Jin had bought, but it didn't have a consort bond's energy to draw on. I'd tried to bolster it as well as I could despite that, but obviously I hadn't shielded him enough.

"I'm okay," he said quickly, squeezing my hand and giving me a smile. "Promise. It was more the surprise than anything. They really like to hit us out of nowhere, don't they?"

He sounded steady enough. "Yeah," I muttered. "They do." That was one in the long list of things I could say I really didn't like about the Assembly, or at least the faction of them that was after us.

They seemed to be done for now, though. I waited through the thump of my pulse, but no more magic followed the last spell I'd fended off.

With a sigh, I leaned my head against Gabriel's shoulder, breathing in the darkly sweet smell of him. He slid his arm around my back. Sitting there nestled against him, I could almost imagine a future less fraught.

"You've traveled all over the place," I said. "Is there anywhere you've been that you think would make a good spot for a witch and her illicit consorts to disappear to?"

Gabriel hummed to himself thoughtfully. "There are a lot of little hole-in-the-wall places in California. And quite a lot of liberal-minded people who might not think our relationship was *that* bizarre." He grinned. "I don't know what kind of presence your witching society has down that way, though."

"There are some witching communities in the south, but most of the families ended up gathering around the north and east coasts," I said. "I don't think it would be too hard to avoid notice. I guess I'd have to change my appearance—maybe bleach my hair."

Damon made a disgruntled sound from up front. "You shouldn't have to change anything."

"I shouldn't, but that doesn't mean I don't." I fingered a smooth black lock. "If changing a few things like that means we can have a real life..."

"We could find another fixer upper down there," Jin said. "Seth could work his kind of magic on it."

A pang shot through me at the thought of the house Seth had already made over for us: that farmhouse just across the road from the Hallowell estate. But the chances we'd ever get to go back there were slim. And this dream was a nice one.

"A little place in the country," I said. "Lots of land to roam around on without anyone disturbing our privacy."

"I can always find work online," Kyler said. "And Jin could travel around to sell his art. Seth could start his own renovation business—or stick to odd jobs to keep a lower profile. Gabriel, you've got your mechanic's touch. That'll always be in demand."

"And I'll sit around with Rose all day," Damon declared.

We all laughed, quietly to avoid waking up Seth. "I'm sure you'd find some way to occupy yourself," I teased. "Maybe you'd find you enjoy farming. *I* definitely wouldn't want to just sit around." I'd been working on the witching archive's records and compiling my own modern history. Obviously I'd have to set that aside. But I could use those skills in other ways.

Damon and Jin started discussing our next possible

stop along the route. I tipped my head against Gabriel's shoulder.

"It's a nice dream, isn't it?" he said, hugging me closer.

"It is." The thought of that possible future had left me with a warm glow. "Maybe it won't be a dream."

"With you, I'd believe just about anything's possible."

He traced his fingers up and down my side, and a tingle of deeper warmth raced through me. I looked up at him, and he gazed back at me, his expression so fond that I couldn't stop myself from easing up to press my lips to his.

Gabriel kissed me back gently at first and then, when I deepened the kiss, with a passion that seared from his mouth to mine. His hand stroked from my hip to my knee and back again, leaving my skin quivering eagerly in its wake. I ran my fingers into his hair, kissing him even harder.

I wanted more of him—more heat, more sweetness, more passion. It was only a few days ago that we'd first really come together. I wanted him and loved him just as much as the other guys. I just needed to be sure he knew that.

But he stopped, lowering his head so our lips eased apart. His breath was ragged in the space between us.

"This doesn't make sense," he murmured. "I'm not the one you need right now. You've been using so much magic, and I can't help you kindle more."

The rough note in his voice carried desire and something more wrenching. He didn't need to tell me he wished he could offer me that too. I could almost taste his frustration.

"It doesn't matter," I said. "I want you too. I never want anything we do to be just about my magic."

"I know," he said. "But you wore yourself out so badly getting us out of that prison, and you must be using a lot shielding us now."

I couldn't deny that a faint ache had started to form around my spark with the last few spells I'd cast. I grimaced, trying to figure out how to turn this conversation in a direction I liked.

Then Ky cleared his throat meaningfully. He leaned around the side of the middle seat to meet my gaze, a mischievous glint in his gray-green eyes.

"Not to eavesdrop, but, ah, I'd be happy to join in the fun and contribute some magical replenishing."

An even headier quiver of desire ran through me. I glanced at Gabriel and found him smiling. If the only way he'd accept my affection right now was with someone else along for the ride, well... I was pretty sure I'd enjoy that ride.

I wet my lips and looked back to Kyler. "All right. I don't think I can argue with an offer that enticing."

He grinned and released his seatbelt. Careful not to disturb his sleeping twin, he ducked around to join us. I undid mine too. I eased over as Kyler sat down, and ended up sitting on Gabriel's lap with my legs sprawled over Ky's. The car bumped over a pothole, settling me even more firmly onto the hard length I could feel against my hip. Gabriel sounded as if he'd swallowed a groan.

"I completely approve of this position," he

murmured, and dipped his head to press his mouth to the side of my neck with a light grazing of teeth. The sensation, tender and slightly sharp, sent an eager quiver over my skin.

"Where do you want me?" Ky asked in a low voice that was so seductive it should have been illegal. I ran my hand down his arm, feeling the lean muscles there.

"Everywhere I can have you," I said.

His laugh was shaky with hunger. "We have to start somewhere. How about... here?"

He reached for the buttons of the blouse I'd bought this morning. His fingertips skimmed my chest as he undid one and then another while Gabriel teased his teeth from my jaw to the crook of my shoulder. My spark flickered at Ky's touch, but Gabriel's caresses burned in their own way.

I shifted my ass against his erection, on purpose this time, and he couldn't restrain that groan. His teeth clamped down a little harder, and a gasp escaped me. At the same moment, Ky slipped his hand beneath my bra. I sighed as he cupped my breast. Bliss sang through my veins, and my spark flared at the intimate contact.

I turned my head to catch Gabriel's mouth with mine. There was no holding back in his kiss now, just raw longing. As our tongues tangled, Ky lifted my shirt and bent down to suck my nipple into his mouth. His fingers eased up my inner thigh to stroke between my legs.

With a whimper, I arched into his touch, bracing one hand against the back of the middle seat. Ky flicked his tongue over the peak of my breast and his thumb over my clit through my jeans, and if my panties had been damp before, they were soaking now.

I teased my fingers into Ky's wild curls, tracing over his scalp. My other hand dropped from the seat to press against Gabriel's cock more firmly. "Fuck," he muttered against my mouth.

I wanted to. By all things lit and warm, did I want to. I tore my lips from his just for a second. "My pants. Off."

Kyler deftly undid my fly, and he and Gabriel tugged my jeans off together in one swift tug. They landed in a heap on the floor of the SUV. Before I could decide the best way to accommodate them both, one way or another, Gabriel lifted me off him and turned me toward Ky. I straddled my consort and glanced back toward the guy who wasn't one.

Gabriel unzipped his jeans. "I can take care of myself," he said, his voice husky. "I want to watch you light up like you're meant to."

I couldn't protest when he said it like that. And when I could feel Ky's firm erection just a few layers of fabric away from the hungriest part of me. I leaned over to give Gabriel one last quick kiss, and then I focused all my attention on my consort.

Kyler traced his thumb over my lips and then drew me to him. He stroked my other breast as we kissed, softly and then sloppily as I started to rock against him on the leather seat.

I fumbled with the zipper of his slacks. He wrenched them down and pulled me against him, nothing but my drenched panties and the soft fabric of his boxers between us now. I pressed into him, every part of me from head to toe, from the surface of my skin to the spark at my core, wanting him.

"So, you want me everywhere, huh?" he murmured. His hands glided over me, spreading electricity over my shoulders, my sides, my calves, even my feet. He kissed his way down my chest and then back to my throat. A swipe of his tongue left me moaning. Ky might be the least experienced of my consorts, but he more than made up for it with enthusiasm and being a quick study.

"Everywhere," I reminded him, and tugged at his boxers. With a chuckle, he shifted against the seat to yank them low enough to free his long, jutting cock. I caressed and squeezed that straining length, and his breath stuttered.

I squirmed out of my panties and lowered myself over Ky. He groaned again as he filled me, and beside us Gabriel made a slightly choked sound. His clothes rustled as he stroked himself, but I was looking only at Ky now. At the heat of love and lust in his eyes as he thrust up to meet me. At the flush spreading over his freckled cheeks that matched the heat building inside me.

"Harder," I whispered. "Faster." I bobbed up and down, my thighs burning, wanting to feel him everywhere inside me too. Pleasure rippled through my body and twined with the bonfire of my spark. The car sped up over a small hill, the motion adding to my exhilaration.

Ky bucked with me, pulling me in for another kiss as he did. He tipped his body and suddenly my clit was bumping against the base of his cock. Headier pulses of bliss shot through me. My rhythm turned frantic. His fingers dug into my hip. Then as he thrust even harder into me, ecstasy burst through my veins.

I muffled my cry against his shoulder, still moving, wanting to milk the pleasure from him too. It didn't take long. Ky inhaled sharply, and I felt him come with a hot spurt inside me.

I came to a stop over him as his cock softened inside me. He wrapped his arms around me, kissing my lips, my cheek, my shoulder, and that tender display of affection stoked my spark even higher. Gabriel swore under his breath with a soft grunt, and I knew he'd found his release too.

The SUV rattled over pebbles on the road. It wasn't really safe staying like this any longer than we needed to. My spark was glowing so bright I could feel it all through my body, but I might need to use that energy again soon.

I let myself linger against Ky for a few seconds longer. He nuzzled my cheek with a smile. "Good?"

I had to laugh. "I hope you don't really need to ask that."

Reluctantly, I peeled myself off him. When my gaze found Gabriel's again, his bright blue eyes were even more brilliant than usual. I retrieved my panties and jeans off the floor and scrambled into them as quickly as I could in the tight space. Ky hauled up his pants and gave me a final kiss before he returned to his seat to give me back mine.

I sat down, sagging into the padded leather surface for a moment of relaxation with my shoulder pressed comfortably against Gabriel's. I was only just reaching for my seatbelt when a blast of magic slammed into us—and the SUV.

The tires screeched. Damon gave a shout, yanking at the wheel. But the vehicle swayed, and with a stomach-dropping lurch we tipped right over.

CHAPTER NINE

Rose

The side of the SUV hit the road like a thunderclap, a crash of metal and splintering glass. The impact flung me into Gabriel, who threw his arms around me just in time to stop my head from smacking into the shattered window now beneath us. His torso jerked against his seatbelt.

Somewhere ahead of us Damon was cursing up a storm and someone—Seth? Oh, dear Spark, he hadn't been buckled in either while he slept— let out a groan.

Another wave of magic slammed into the car, rocking it. Gabriel hissed through his teeth. Even I felt it through the layers of protection I'd woven around myself: little shards of pain as if the magic were echoing the broken glass beneath me.

I scrambled around, trying to get my bearings while my head spun—and trying not to hurt Gabriel more in the process. Where were the attacks coming from? How close were the enforcers now? I stretched out my senses as my feet crunched on the remains of the window and registered the next blast of energy emanating from a cluster of bodies farther down the road on both sides.

They didn't feel quite the same as the witches who'd been attacking us before. The faction that was after us had gotten ahead of us, sent a force to ambush us while distracting us with lesser assaults.

I swept my arms to draw up a barrier of magic between us and them, but it was hard to move at all in the toppled car. I had no idea how long that effort would hold.

"I need to get out so I can work properly," I said. "The rest of you might be safer out of the SUV too, in case we need to run for it."

"Got it," Kyler said with a rasp. On the side of the SUV that was now above us, he heaved at the door. It swung open on his second attempt. Gabriel shifted beside me and offered his hands to boost me up.

Jin was shoving his way out at the front, Damon waiting to clamber after him. "Seth?" I said as I grabbed the doorframe and hauled myself up. I hadn't seen him yet, hadn't heard him except for that groan.

"I'll help him," Ky said quickly. "You stop those pricks out there."

My heart wrenched, but stopping the enforcers was the best way I could keep Seth safe until I had time to heal whatever injuries he'd suffered. Gritting my teeth, I squirmed the rest of the way out.

"They're to the west," I called to the others as I slid

down to the road. "Get behind the SUV. It'll shield us a little."

I darted behind it myself and immediately threw myself into a larger magicking, now that I had the room for it. My feet pattered against the asphalt, and the air whipped with the slash of my arms. I focused my attention on those clusters of figures ahead of us.

It wasn't enough just to shield us. The closer they got, the harder they'd hit us, and there were a lot more of them than me. But my spark was freshly flaring and I'd die before I let them take me or my guys again.

With one last snap of my wrists, I hurled a surge of power toward our attackers. Knock them down, knock them out, I didn't care as long as I got them to back off. The wind warbled around us, and a distant cry reached my ears. A few of the presences I'd sensed faded.

How hard had I hit them? Had I *killed* someone? The thought sent a shock of cold horror through me. But before I could deal with that, the remaining enforcers tossed another spell our way. A sizzling impression of a vast net hurtled toward us.

No! I pushed forth my magic, launching every movement I knew to sever and shatter. Energy rushed through my limbs. I propelled it out and felt the thrust of the enforcers' spell crack just as it plummeted to meet us.

It broke apart, but the slivers of energy burned as they dropped around me. I flinched back, almost bumping into Jin. He and Damon had joined me.

"Where are the others?" I asked breathlessly.

"Gabriel and Kyler are looking after Seth," Jin said. When my eyes widened, he added quickly, "He took a blow to the head, but it's not bleeding much, and he's coherent. Nothing unfixable."

He couldn't know that for sure, but the words soothed my panic a little.

Damon cracked his knuckles. One of the shreds of the magical net had brushed his cheek, leaving a red mark, but he didn't look bothered. "How do we take the bastards down, Rose?"

I dragged in a breath. "I've got to hit them again before they hit us." And even harder than last time. And if I did more than knock them out... I couldn't worry about that right now. I didn't want to kill anyone, but that didn't matter half as much as making sure they didn't kill us.

Damon clasped my waist, hugging me partly from behind. He kissed my shoulder. "Right here with you, angel. Take anything you need."

Jin slung his arm around my back too, pressing his lips to my temple. The consort bond between us thrummed, and my spark shot up with a blaze of light. A strange giddiness rippled through me.

I had my consorts, their love feeding my magic. My love for them made me stronger than any of those enforcers could have imagined. I clasped onto that blaze inside me and whirled my arms through the air, gathering it and balling it together until the air rang with the power I held. Then I whipped it down the road.

The spell exploded through our attackers with a force that rattled the ground beneath our feet. I would have stumbled if Damon and Jin hadn't still been holding me.

My impression of the figures down the road

completely dimmed. Whatever I'd managed to do to them, they weren't going to come at us again right now.

I exhaled shakily and squeezed the guys' arms. Then I tugged them with me to the toppled SUV.

Ky and Gabriel were just easing Seth out through the doorway. The larger guy swayed a little as he clutched the frame, but he met my gaze steadily and smiled when he saw me. A purple-red bruise was spreading across his temple around a cut still seeping blood. My stomach turned at the sight of it.

I held out my hand as Gabriel hopped down. Seth grasped it and slid the rest of the way to the pavement with Gabriel bracing his other arm. Seth tested his balance on his feet and then pulled me into a massive hug.

"You're okay," he said.

"*I'm* okay?" I said. "Look at you. Get over here. I'll patch you up as well as I can. You could have a concussion."

He grimaced, but he walked with us to the side of the road. I knelt beside him, studying the wound. I'd studied plenty of healing spells—they were some of the most generally useful magic any witch could learn, so my tutors had spent a lot of time on them—but I hadn't needed to cast anything major in the short time I'd actually had my magic. And you always had to be careful when manipulating someone's body in any way.

I murmured a few focusing words under my breath and moved my fingers through the air over Seth's temple in a delicate dance. Seal the skin, ease any swelling, numb the pain. The aches in my own body started to throb as I spun the careful spells. Gabriel might have saved me from the worst of the impact, but I'd banged myself up a fair bit.

When I finished, Seth's skin was still bruised, but the cut was closed. He touched the spot gingerly and gave a hoarse chuckle. "It hardly even hurts. I'd say it's like magic, but it actually was magic."

"If you can make a joke like that, you really must be feeling better." The urge gripped me, and I had to lean in to kiss him. "Don't you ever get bashed up like that again," I ordered him, my hands cupping his face and my nose brushing his.

He ran his thumb over my cheek. "I'll do my best."

I straightened up and glanced over the other guys. They all looked a tad dazed, but that wasn't exactly surprising after what we'd just been through. Damon had taken that burn from the magical net, and his left elbow looked bruised. Gabriel's arm was scratched where it must have collided with the window, but nothing deep. Ky and Jin seemed to have made it out pretty much unscathed.

I motioned Gabriel over. "You don't have to—" he started as I took his arm, and I silenced him with a pointed look.

"Tell yourself you're doing me a favor," I said. "I'm going to be distracted as long as any of you are bleeding."

He laughed. "All right, fine. But we don't know if more of those Assembly assholes might be on their way, do we? We should get out of here fast."

I couldn't argue with that. My gut tightened as I worked a spell to knit his skin. When I stepped back, my spark was still blazing merrily inside me, but nowhere near as hotly as before.

I wasn't worn out, no, but I was already on my way there. The tightness in my gut turned into a heavy stone that sank even deeper.

"I don't think this is going to work."

"What do you mean?" Ky asked.

"The whole idea of running away and finding some place to hide out... I don't know if we can ever get far enough ahead of them to put down roots somewhere." That dream we'd only just talked about had shattered like the car's windows. I swallowed hard. "And I know for sure I won't be able to keep this up indefinitely. I'm not omnipotent, as much as I'd like to be right now."

"Well, we're sure as hell not letting them *win*," Damon said.

Gabriel nodded. "What did you have in mind, Rose?"

He watched me with that assured calm he never seemed to lose—except for that one moment a few days ago when he'd broken down and admitted to me how broken he felt. He'd said he believed in me. Was he really that confident, all the way through, that I could get us out of this?

I had to believe that he was. *I* had to believe in me. The guys I'd brought into this dangerous witching world didn't have anyone else to see them through it.

"If we can't keep running," I said, "then the only other option I can see is to fight. Whatever ways we can. Scare them, hurt them... Expose them to the rest of witching society if we can. If we can't, at least make them believe they're better off letting us go live our lives than keeping up the fight on their end."

"I'm all for that," Jin said. "How do we get started?"

"That's the big question." I let out a halting laugh. "Before we can strike back, I think we need a better idea of who we're dealing with. Where they're vulnerable. What proof we can gather." I glanced down the road. "You know, there was a witch in New York City I talked to—Margo Elands. She'd researched some of the less-known witching history and gotten in trouble with the Assembly for talking about things they wanted to keep quiet. Maybe she'd be able to help us." She might have something on them she hadn't wanted to use herself. *Her life wasn't on the line.*

"New York's a long way away," Seth said.

"I know. But there's also..." An odd sensation stirred in my chest, like hope and anxiety twisted together. "My mother's family is out there. I haven't seen them since I was a little kid. I don't know how much they even remember me. But they didn't like my dad. Maybe they had some idea what kind of person he was. They might help us against him and his allies too."

"New York it is, then," Damon said with a clap of his hands. "We'd better get moving."

Seth glanced at the toppled SUV. "On foot?"

I looked down the lonely highway and bit my lip. We'd purposely been sticking to more isolated roads, but now that could be a problem. No one had passed us since the crash. It could be a long way to the next town.

"It's still on the road," I said, nodding to the SUV.

"Do you think the five of you could manage to push it back onto its wheels if I add some magic to the mix?"

"Can't hurt to try," Gabriel said. "The engine might be a problem." He nudged Damon. "Was it still running when we tipped?"

Damon shook his head. "I remembered what you said. As soon as I could tell we were going to crash, I switched it off."

"That gives us a better chance. Come on."

He motioned us all over to the sideways roof of the SUV. The guys bent down and fit their fingers into the best holds they could find.

"On a count of three," Gabriel said. "Three, two..."

I was already moving, shifting magic through me and toward the car. As Gabriel said, "One!" and the guys heaved at the frame, I shoved at it with a force of my own.

The SUV lurched upright, settling onto its wheels with a heavy thud.

For a second we all just stood there, breathing hard. I peered at the windows while Gabriel started inspecting the tires. The glass all along the left side of the car was shattered, but the rest were fine.

"I don't think I can meld the glass back together." I toed the shards on the ground. "But I can put up a simple illusion that'll stop anyone from realizing they're broken. It's warm enough that it shouldn't matter having some air come in, right?"

"Sounds reasonable to me," Ky said.

"The tires look okay," Gabriel said. "The real question is whether that engine is going to start."

He lifted the hood and looked it over. "This isn't the

happiest looking system I've ever seen. But maybe..." He reached inside, twisted something, fiddled with something else. Then he pulled back, shut the hood, and held out his hand for Damon to pass him the key.

My throat tightened as he hopped into the driver's seat. If this didn't work...

Gabriel turned the key. The engine sputtered—and then thrummed to life. My shoulders sagged in relief.

Knocking the last few slivers of glass away from the side window, Gabriel leaned out his elbow and turned to grin at us. "Everybody back in! Let's see what New York has in store."

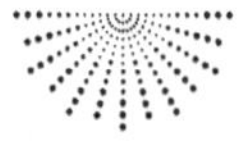

CHAPTER TEN

Kyler

The moon was full overhead, the night air cool on my skin, when Damon and I swapped off spots at the front of the SUV with Seth and Gabriel in the wee hours of the morning. I peered up at the gleaming circle against the near-black sky. "Well, that's not ominous or anything."

"I don't think we need any omens to know we're in a tight situation," my twin said, but he managed to sound a little wry.

"True. Very true." I looked him over. "You're feeling totally okay? No headache, fogginess, or dizziness? Ringing in your ears?"

Seth shook his head at me as he got into the driver's seat. "Why do I have the feeling you've been scouring the internet for symptoms of a concussion? I'm fine, Ky." He glanced back at me to catch my eyes. "I promise."

I held up my hands. "Hey, I had to ask. The last thing we need is you out of commission."

Rose was still dozing in the middle row of seats, her jacket bunched under her head. When I slid in next to her, she roused enough to reach over and squeeze my hand. I squeezed her fingers in return. The sight of her, tired and probably a little frayed but able to relax for now, made my chest fill with so much affection that I almost thought it would burst.

I'd have liked to snuggle up with her and fall into my own doze, but instead I pulled out the stolen phone. Rose had worn herself ragged protecting us. I'd better do my bit to protect her.

Damon sank into the seat next to me. "What're you doing with that thing now?" he asked, keeping his voice low. Jin was sleeping in the back. The car rumbled as Seth hit the gas.

"I'm still working on finding a back door into the Assembly's server," I said. My thumb skimmed over the touch screen. "I've tried a few things that didn't work out, but I've got another strategy that I've made some progress with."

He snorted. "I thought you could hack your way into anything in two seconds flat."

"Not quite," I said with a laugh. "Getting into the *phone* wasn't hard. And it's been used to access at least one level of the Assembly's database before. But they cancelled her user account as soon as they realized the phone was stolen, it looks like. So I've got to carve my own way in."

"Hmm. Yeah. I wouldn't know where to start.

Haven't really had time to play around with computers a whole lot."

Because he'd been busy getting in trouble in class and then working sketchy jobs to keep afloat after he'd dropped out of high school. Yeah, I guessed my honor roll, college graduate self must look pretty privileged to him.

We'd all suffered some when Rose's dad had fired our parents from the Hallowell estate staff as punishment for the friendship we'd formed with her all those years ago, but my and Seth's parents had found their feet pretty quickly. Whenever I'd seen Damon's mom around town, she'd always looked run down and sad. And his dad had run off years before that.

He hadn't sounded pissed about it just now, but a prickle of guilt ran through my gut anyway. "I'm sorry," I said.

Damon raised his eyebrows at me. "For what? My lack of computer skills?"

Oh, hell, I was probably going to put my foot in it. But I'd already committed.

"I just mean—back then. All the stuff you were going through. I wish I'd reached out more. I mean, we used to be best friends, all five of us... We didn't have to drift apart. I should have tried harder."

Damon blinked at me. He ducked his head, his spiky coffee-brown hair drifting to shadow his eyes. "I guess I can't say I was doing a whole lot of reaching out myself."

"You were having a hard time," I said. "I knew that. I wish I'd done more. That's all." I paused. "Although maybe it was for the best in the end, because if you *hadn't* gone off and made those new friends of yours, you wouldn't have picked up all the nifty breaking-and-entering skills we've found so useful."

I wanted to take the words back the second they'd spilled from my mouth. Yeah, that didn't sound at all insensitive or anything. Damon's head jerked up so he could stare at me, and I gulped. His mouth twisted.

Then he started to laugh.

The sound was catching. In a second, I was laughing too. The comment hadn't even been that funny, but it was a relief just to feel like we could laugh about something in the middle of all this.

"You do have an interesting way of looking at things, Mr. Brainiac," Damon said when he'd caught his breath. "I guess that's for the best too. Get on with your fancy-pants hacking."

He leaned back in his seat, letting his eyes drift shut. As I tapped into the interface I'd been using, Rose stirred at my other side. "What's so funny?" she murmured.

"Nothing really," I said, still smiling. "Nothing worth waking up for, anyway."

She made a dismissive noise. After a swivel of her hand, her body went unnaturally still for a moment. When I glanced over at her, wondering what spell she'd cast, she nodded.

"I can't sense any magic at all anywhere nearby. I don't know how much range I have, but I think the way I'm checking now, I'd know if they were close enough to really hurt us." She sighed. "I guess tonight's attack was their big effort."

"They're regrouping," I suggested.

"We've got to assume so. I don't think they're going to back down yet."

It'd be easier to know if I could get into this damn server. My fingers flicked over the screen. A little code here. Massage a password there. Chip away at the walls around the network until I had a hole just big enough to weasel my way in.

I'd broken into a whole lot of secure databases in my time: banks, government, you name it. Just for kicks, though. None of them had really mattered.

Breaking through *these* layers of security, on the other hand, could be a matter of life and death.

I squinted at the screen, tapping out another sequence on the touchscreen keyboard. This wasn't exactly the greatest phone I'd ever worked with either. But—hey! Was that an opening?

My spirits shot up. My fingers dashed over the screen as if the crack I'd discovered might close at any second. I shoved it wider with another line of code, and— bingo! The lowest level of the Assembly's private database spilled down the screen. My mouth stretched into a grin.

Ha. They might have magic, but they didn't rule the internet, that was for sure.

My excitement must have radiated off me a little more strongly than I'd intended, because Rose shifted again, tipping her head against my shoulder and looking down at the screen. "Is that good?" she asked, looking hazily at the interface.

"I just got into the low security level of the Assembly's network," I said. "I don't think I'll be able to access the super secure areas from the phone, but we'll have access to their basic records now."

She scooted a little closer, her expression becoming more alert. "That's great! I don't even know what we should look up at this point, though. The faction that's hunting us will have kept all *their* records separate."

I nodded. "I'd probably have to be physically in their building to have much chance at those." Even sitting in the coffee shop across the street a few weeks ago, they'd shut me down before I'd grabbed more than a couple of files. But we could use this entry point in other ways. "I know the names I saw on the form I dug up—the one where they approved the murder of that witch and her lover. And we know your father and that Frankford guy are involved too."

"And my stepmother," Rose said. She winced. "Or at least she was."

Because Celestine Hallowell had recently become the victim of another highly suspicious accident. This faction of the Assembly had used a supposed car crash to cover up things they didn't want getting out before. What were the chances she'd just happened to get hit, right after Rose had sent her running from the estate? Right before she'd been supposed to carry out Mr. Hallowell's dirty work, binding Rose in that corrupted consorting?

But that didn't mean her name wouldn't be useful. "Right," I said. "I can cross-reference those names with any of the witches you think we could turn to for help. See if I come across any connections between them, good or bad. So we can be a little more sure that they're not under the influence of this group in any way."

"That's a good idea." She looped her arm around mine in a gesture so comfortably familiar another pang of affection shot through me. "The first person I figured we should talk to is Margo Elands. I texted her from the burner phone you got me back when I was trying to figure out whether I even could kindle my spark properly with consorts who weren't witching men."

"She'd heard about other witches doing that?" I said, my eyebrows rising.

Rose shook her head. "Not any time recently. Just, like, a legend sort of thing. From what I read, she dabbles in the more obscure or questionable areas of witching history. And she'd seen a few of those etchings like the ones in the tower on my property—pictures of witches with multiple consorts. Apparently she'd mentioned those tidbits of history in the wrong company, and it got her fired from a job with the Assembly. She owns a New Age shop on Staten Island now."

"She definitely sounds like someone who might be on our side, then. Let me see what I can find on her."

I started a search of the database looking for any documents in the vast array that contained both Margo Eland's name and any of the witching people we knew were part of the conspiracy.

"I'm not seeing anything about her in the database," I said. "Let me try regular old Google too." They might be witches, but they had real lives in the real world that could intersect in different ways.

Nothing came up there either. "Ms. Eland seems clean," I said. "I mean, we'll still want to be cautious, but

I don't see any reason to worry about her somehow being involved with that shady faction."

"Yeah, that seemed pretty unlikely anyway," Rose said.

I looked at her. "You were thinking maybe we could contact your mom's family too, right?"

"Yeah." She hesitated. "I've never even talked to them before... My dad always made it seem like they disowned *us* because they weren't happy about the marriage. I figured they were all snobby jerks. But now I've got to wonder if he pushed them away because they knew something wasn't totally right with him. I'm not even sure... What if he did something to my mom like he meant to have happen between Derek and me? What if he was controlling her magic?"

What if he'd been responsible for her death too? She didn't have to ask that question—it hung in the air regardless.

"I wouldn't be surprised," I said to the questions she *had* asked. "I can see if there's anything to dig up here. What's their family name?"

"Levesque," she said. "That was her maiden name. Alora Levesque. I found an old photo once of her with her sisters—the older one was Irene and the younger one was Virginia. I don't know about her parents, or any kids my aunts might have now..."

"That's fine," I said. "That's enough."

I started by searching for Irene and Virginia Levesque in the New York City area. It didn't take long to find a large property on the outskirts of one of the particularly posh suburbs. Irene held that one. And Virginia's name was on the deed of a slightly smaller estate just a mile away.

"It looks like they're still in New York State," I said. "And close to each other. Let's see what else I can find…"

My digging turned up almost as much nothing as when I'd looked for Margo Elands.

"There are a couple of records in the Assembly's database," I told Rose. "A while back Virginia filed a minor dispute with Frankford about the tutor she hired on the Education division's recommendation. It looks like she has a daughter who's just a couple years younger than you. And Irene and your father served on a board together for a year, about thirty years ago. I'm going to guess that was how he ended up meeting your mother. I don't see any sign that the two of them had any connection other than that."

"Hard to tell without being able to access the deeper records, though, right?" Rose said.

"Yeah. I can't be sure. Even with those we couldn't be perfectly sure." I ran my hand over my hair, the curls scattering under my fingers. "But if anyone from your mother's family was on your father's side, you'd think he'd have brought them back into your life. Another point of influence."

"That's true." Rose rubbed her mouth. "At least we know where to find them now."

That didn't feel like enough. I frowned at the phone. Then something Gabriel had mentioned earlier came back to me. The enforcers who'd been holding us—one of them had said something to him about a "Cliff."

A search of the Assembly's database turned up nothing. I switched to the regular internet. First I checked for "Maxim Hallowell" and then "Charles Frankford." My thumbs stilled over the screen.

"Did you find something?" Rose asked, leaning closer.

"I don't know." I cocked my head as I considered the article I'd found. "It's just a little piece from some small-town paper... So small I guess this qualified as news. It's reporting that Charles Frankford the First purchased a large property near the coast there, 'just east of the cliff area.' The First? It's from fifty years ago."

"Maybe the dad of the Frankford I've met? Or his grandfather? What's the name of the town?"

"Heronville."

"Nope, definitely never heard anything significant about that." Rose's brow knit. "Maybe that's something to look into if we can't dig up anything else to help us, though."

"Yeah."

"But not right now," Seth's voice carried from the front. "You two are supposed to be getting some sleep, remember? We want to be fresh for whatever the Assembly throws at us tomorrow."

Rose made a face. "He's right," she said. "Come here."

She nestled against me, inviting me to lean my head against hers. I let myself relax into her the way I'd longed to earlier, because Seth was right. I needed my mind sharp. And I'd already found out a lot.

But under the warm flush of victory, my nerves

weren't exactly calm. We might have allies in Rose's mother's family, but what had happened between them and her dad in the first place? And what did this Cliff have to do with anything?

Nothing good—that was all I knew for sure.

CHAPTER ELEVEN

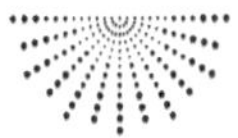

Rose

"So you said Margo Elands's shop is on Staten Island?" Gabriel said. He was at the wheel of the SUV now. It was late afternoon, and we'd just come into the built-up area around New York City proper.

I rubbed my eyes. I'd gotten some sleep here and there overnight and through the day's long drive, but I couldn't say I really felt rested. Especially since I'd been reaching out with my magic over and over, testing for the presence of other spells in opposition.

Just in the last few hours, I'd started to feel a faint tingling. Distant still and not an overt attack, but enough to put me on my guard. The Assembly was still searching for us. I couldn't be sure how closely they were tracking us.

"That's right," I said. "I've got the address. I can give you directions once we get over there."

"Looks like we'll reach the bridge in about ten minutes," Kyler said from where he was navigating from the phone.

Behind me, Damon leaned his arm out the open window. "I want to head over to Brooklyn for a bit. There are a few guys there I know. They might be able to help out in non-magical ways."

"Like what?" I asked, tensing a little, both at the idea of one of my consorts leaving the group even for a little while—and at the idea of what Damon might have planned. He'd calmed down some since I'd first gotten back in town, but he still had some... overly aggressive ideas of how to deal with problems. He'd sent a bunch of small-time gangsters to beat up Derek when my former fiancé had been getting overly pushy with me, even though I'd had the situation under control.

"Nothing you need to worry about," he said in his favorite cocky tone. "I'll just be getting some supplies. I promise I won't get anyone else involved."

Well, I guessed that was something. "I don't think you should go alone," I said.

"These kind of guys don't really want a whole party of people they don't know showing up on their doorstep."

"Can you at least take *someone*, just in case trouble shows up?" I wasn't sure what any of the guys could do against the enforcers on their own, but at least if two of them were together, they had more of a chance of creating a distraction or getting a message to me so I could help.

"I wouldn't mind seeing more of the city," Kyler piped up before Damon could argue with me. "I could use some supplies too—see if I can come up with some tech for getting through all the Assembly's internal security, if we ever have the chance to take a real go at the deeper layers of their network."

Damon sighed. "All right, all right. But you're hanging back while I'm actually talking with these guys."

Ky raised his hands. "No argument there. The low-lifes are all yours."

Damon snorted a laugh, and Ky grinned. Sometime last night they'd gotten a little friendlier. I'd have been happier to see it if my stomach wasn't still twisted up at the thought of them leaving my side at all.

But the enforcers hadn't really hurt the guys even when they'd had us all locked up before. After they'd crashed the van, their spells had been aimed more to capture us than destroy us. They were protecting *me* for whatever reason. I could hope they'd at least continue that policy.

"Do you have enough money for these supplies?" I asked, reaching for the purse where I'd stashed all the cash I'd taken out.

"I cleared out my account," Damon said. "I'm set for a while. I won't be getting too fancy, angel."

The twist in my stomach tightened with a pinch of guilt. One more way their association with me was changing all of their lives. I didn't want them losing everything. Maybe it was silly to think that way about money when our actual lives were on the line, but they wouldn't have been risking anything at all if it wasn't for me.

Seth reached over from where he was sitting beside

me and squeezed my knee as if he'd sensed my thoughts. They wanted to be here, I reminded myself. With every action and every word, they proved how true that was.

"It's not just for you, so it shouldn't all come out of your wallet," I said. I fished out a wad of hundreds and handed it back to him.

"Rose," Damon said.

I shook my head. "You're taking it. To make me feel better. Come on." I shook the bills at him.

He grumbled wordlessly, but he took the cash.

"You too," I said, handing some to Kyler. He raised an eyebrow at me as if to say I should know it wasn't necessary but took the money without protest.

"I can think of a few uses I could put this to."

We cruised over the bridge and down the wide, sparsely treed streets of Staten Island. As we reached the main commercial strip, I motioned for Gabriel to stop.

A fresh wave of that eerie tingling washed over me again. Distant, yeah, but I wasn't sure I could even trust my sense of its source. The enforcers had taken us by surprise before.

"It's just a few more blocks," I said. "We can walk the rest of the way."

Gabriel parked by the curb. Damon and Ky hopped out right away, Damon grabbing me for a quick kiss.

"We meet back here," I said. "Or I'll text you on your burner if we have to head somewhere else. And you tell me if you see anything suspicious."

"Yes, ma'am," Damon said dryly. He gave Ky a light shove toward the road and flagged a cab.

"Should someone stay with the car?" Jin asked, leaning against the back of the middle row of seats.

I wavered. "No. I want you guys with me if anything happens. We can stand to lose the car."

I hefted my purse over my shoulder. With Jin, Gabriel, and Seth gathered around me, we set off down the street. I counted off the numbers as we approached the spot where Margo Elands's New Age shop should be.

The website had prepared me for the garish purple-and-green sign and the twinkling of crystals in the window. It hadn't prepared me for the CLOSED sign hanging on the door.

My legs jerked to a halt. I scooted to the side to be out of the late afternoon just-got-out-of-work foot traffic. The guys gathered around me as I peered into the dark space beyond the window. A whiff of resin-tinged incense carried through the door, but nothing moved among the shelves of tarot cards and multi-colored candles on the other side.

"The website said the store is open until eight," I said. My gaze dropped to the letters printed on the glass. The hours there were exactly the same.

"Maybe she's changed things up and hasn't had time to edit the website?" Jin suggested. "Or the door?"

I bit my lip. I hadn't texted Margo ahead of time because I didn't know if the Assembly might be keeping an eye on her because of her past behavior. If I'd given them any hint we were coming to see her, though...

"What if they figured out we were coming this way?" I said. "What if the Assembly has already come after her?"

Gabriel frowned. "Then they'd have been here waiting for us to show, wouldn't they? They'd have already grabbed us. It could be anything, Rose. She might be taking a sick day or something totally normal like that for all we know."

Seth rubbed my shoulders. "You know I'm not one to be carelessly optimistic," he said. "But I agree with Gabriel. Why don't we come back tomorrow morning and see if she's here then?"

"I'll text her now," I said, pulling out my burner. "Nothing obvious. Just asking when the store will re-open. That shouldn't hurt anything." And at least it'd give me some reassurance she was okay.

"What should we do in the meantime?" Jin asked. "Do you want to reach out to your mother's family right away?"

My pulse skipped a beat. "No," I said. "I don't think it'd be a good idea to extend ourselves too far all at once. Let's wait and see what I hear from Margo—if I hear anything—and then figure out how to approach them. I've never even talked to them, let alone seen them. I don't even know for sure if they know I exist. It's not going to be a simple visit."

"I don't think we can just crash in the SUV overnight," Seth said, glancing back toward our vehicle with a frown of his own.

Gabriel nodded. "Not the kind of thing you can get away with very easily in a big city. What do you think is our safest bet while we wait, Rose?"

"I have a friend in the art scene who has a pad in Manhattan," Jin put in. "He gave me carte blanche to stay there when he's not in town, which is most of the time. He just left for a month-long trip across northern Africa. I don't have the key on me, but we've got magic on our side, so..." He grinned at me.

We could keep driving around until I heard back from Margo—or we could get some real rest. I hesitated. "Let's take a look at this place. I want to be sure we can get out of there quickly if we need to."

I checked my phone for the millionth time as we pulled up outside the building where Jin's friend had his "pad." Damon had confirmed that he and Kyler would head over here when they'd finished their errands, but still nothing from Margo. I resisted the urge to nibble at my lip and peered out the window.

I'd been picturing some Manhattan high-rise, but what I saw actually put me more at ease: a four-story brownstone with a hair salon at its base, an alley beside it, and a fire escape snaking down its brick side. We'd have at least two exit routes, then. And it'd be easy to keep an eye on the street outside to see if anyone was approaching. The enforcers would have to get close to attack us physically in there. They couldn't tip over a whole building like they had the SUV.

A quick spell got us past the front door and then the door for the actual apartment. It was two floors of open-concept space, all creamy walls, leather and ebony furniture, with modern art in stark colors and shapes all over the place. A crisp, slightly ocean-y scent hung in the air. The whole setting was so different from what we'd been living with for the last few days that a slightly hysterical laugh slipped out of me.

"He's got a bit different artistic tastes from you," I said, turning to take in all of the paintings on the walls.

"Yep," Jin said. "Modern to the bone. But we do manage to get along somehow anyway."

There were three bedrooms upstairs. I walked into the first one, took one look at the king-sized bed with its fluffy duvet, and collapsed right into it. For a second, surrounded by feathery softness, I actually felt relaxed.

Gabriel chuckled. "Enjoying yourself, Sprout?"

"I'd be enjoying myself even more if I had company," I said, and then reality caught back up with me. I pushed myself upright and flicked my hand through the air to send out another testing wave of magic. It didn't meet anything at all around us. Even the tingling from before had faded. But we'd been through too much for me to take comfort in that.

"We should keep an eye on the area around the building," I said. "Someone watching the front and the back from the windows at all times."

"Sure," Gabriel said. "But not you. You've worn yourself thin enough as it is. Lie back down and get some rest." He gave me a crooked smile. "At least once in a while I should get to give the orders. I'll take the front window."

I muttered a vague protest, but I didn't really *want* to get up. I flopped back down on the pillow. "I'll keep an eye on the backyard," Jin said. "Nice little balcony back there anyway."

Seth paused by the doorway. "Well," he said, "since it sounds like the surveillance is covered…"

He climbed onto the bed and wrapped his arm around me. I turned to snuggle closer with a happy sigh. My hand traced down his muscular body, easing around the pendant I'd been able to cast a protective spell on during a brief stop for gas this morning. I tipped my head to steal a kiss.

I'd meant it to be just quick and sweet, but as Seth's mouth moved against mine and heat flared through my body, I couldn't remember why I wouldn't have wanted this to last forever.

"Are you up for more?" he murmured against my lips. The huskiness of his voice took my breath away. When I'd gone to check on him in the back seat this morning it had turned into a quick tumble, but it was hard to imagine the hunger I felt for him and all my consorts ever completely fading. Maybe it would ease off a little when our bond wasn't quite so new, but right now I wanted as much of them as I could get.

"Always," I said. Then I pulled back a little farther to search his gray-green eyes, like his twin's but always more serious. "Are you sure *you're* up for it? You were just hurt, and this morning we already—"

He interrupted me by nuzzling my cheek. "I wouldn't offer if I wasn't eager. You know, there's one thing I've been wanting to do that there really wasn't much room for in the car."

Before I could ask what, he was already sliding down my body. His hand opened my jeans and tugged them down in two smooth motions. He kissed my stomach, my hip bone, the sensitive skin just above the band of my panties. A tingle of anticipation shot up from my core. Heat pooled between my legs.

Seth stroked a finger over my clit and down my panties, drawing the wetness of my arousal through the fabric. Then he eased those down too. His breath spilled hot over my sex as he lowered his mouth to me.

I whimpered, clutching at his close-cropped hair, as he swiped his tongue across my clit and lower. His thumb dipped inside my opening. Pleasure spiked through me with each caress of his lips and hand, sending the light of my spark flooding through every nerve.

"Seth," I mumbled. And then I couldn't form any coherent sounds at all. His teeth grazed my clit and his fingers worked deeper inside me, and for a few minutes I was nothing but bliss beneath my consort.

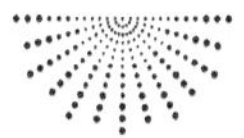

CHAPTER TWELVE

Damon

"She answered!" Rose bounded down the stairs to the lower floor of the apartment with an excited light in her dark green eyes. "Margo Elands. She's all right. She said she can meet me at Wolfe's Pond Park in a couple hours."

I glanced over at my consort with a grin from where I was standing watch by the front window. "Meet *you*? Pretty sure we're all along for the ride, angel."

"I did mention I'd have company. Probably we shouldn't be too obvious about it." She breezed over to give me a quick kiss with an energy that was infectious. I tugged her to me a little harder, stealing a few more seconds with that heavenly mouth. When she drew back, I didn't think it was just excitement flushing her cheeks.

"There's some pizza left from last night," Gabriel said from the back of the apartment, nodding to the fridge.

The greasy cheese smell of the stuff we'd ordered in still lingered in the air. "If you're not too picky about breakfast."

Rose wrinkled her nose as she rolled her shoulders. "Why don't we go out and grab something on the way to the park? I don't like how long we've been hanging out in the same place."

"I haven't seen any creeps out there," I said, jabbing my thumb toward the window.

Kyler looked up from where he'd been sitting at the table with that damn phone of his and a couple other pieces of equipment I didn't understand that he'd picked up yesterday. "Have you gotten a sense of the Assembly people's magic again, Rose?"

She shook her head. "Nothing more than before. But they've obviously got techniques we're not sure of. At least while we're on the move they can't surround us. Has everyone gotten enough sleep after all that driving the last couple days?"

"I'm good," Jin said, arriving at the bottom of the stairs. He smiled languidly, but his eyes looked alert enough. His damp hair was rumpled as if he'd just rubbed a towel over it. "Nothing like a shower after a long time on the road."

"Is Seth up?" Rose asked.

"He's washing up right now." The artist ambled over to Rose and wrapped his arms around her waist from behind, tucking his chin over her shoulder with a contented sigh.

Yeah. Contented. That was definitely the word for the glow that seemed to fill the room with all of us here in her presence. I let the warmth of it sit in my chest for a few beats, just absorbing the sensation.

It was hard to remember when I'd last felt content in the past several years before Rose had returned. Even with those assholes still on our backs, I wouldn't have given this up for anything.

But damn if there wasn't an ache in my chest too, remembering that short time when we'd really thought everything was okay. When we'd had a place that could have been a real home for all of us to share, at least some of the time.

Fucking bastards. They'd taken that from us. They'd taken it from Rose. All because of their stupid prejudices about guys who hadn't happened to be born into one of their exclusive families?

If they thought they were taking anything more from us, they had another thing coming. My gaze dropped to the backpack I'd stuffed my own recent purchases into. If those "enforcers" messed with us again, they were sure as hell going to regret it.

When Seth had joined us, we headed down to the street. I kept scanning the area as we walked, one hand on the strap of the pack I'd slung over my shoulder. Summer was coming up fast, and even in the middle of the morning you could feel it in the sunny warmth rising between the buildings. The smells of fresh baking drew us into a café a few blocks over.

We came out full of scones and croissants, still an hour before the scheduled meeting time. Rather than hail a cab just yet, we ambled on down a few of the quieter side streets.

We'd just crossed the road when an unsettling prickle ran down my back. I glanced around at the same time Rose slowed.

"Where did everybody go?" I said in a low voice. There'd been other pedestrians scattered along both sides of the street a minute ago. Cars cruising past. Now all of the street in my view was empty. Quiet. In a totally unnatural way.

We all stopped, gathering close together. Rose made a quick gesture with her hand. The air vibrated with a hint of the spell she must have cast closing around us. The wooden pendant under my shirt quivered against my chest.

A man stepped out of a side-street, tall and boxy-shouldered, with a hawkish nose and a few streaks of silver in his copper hair. He wore a suit, as if he were going to some fancy business meeting. But I could tell with one look at him that he was part of the Assembly. The bastards practically stunk of snide condescension when they looked at any of us.

"Stop right there," Rose said, her voice firm but with a tremble she couldn't quite quash. I brushed my hand against hers as if to reassure her we were all there with her. My gaze darted along the street.

Several more figures had emerged at either end— mostly women in the athletic-wear I was starting to associate with the Assembly's enforcers, but also a couple other men in similar clothes holding thick batons I guessed held some kind of attack spells.

The hawkish man who'd been approaching us stilled. He clasped his knobby-knuckled hands in front of him.

"I request a parlay," he said.

"A 'parlay' while your attack dogs creep up on us?" I said.

"Just let us go," Rose said. "I don't want to fight you, but you know that I can."

"I don't want to fight either," the man said. "I was simply hoping for the chance to talk with you. To help you understand our position."

Kyler snorted, expressing the disbelief I think we were all feeling.

"I already understand your position," Rose said, an edge coming into her voice. "You want us all trapped or maybe even dead. The Assembly, or at least your faction of it, has made that very clear."

The prick didn't even try to argue. "Perhaps we could come to alternate terms that are more suitable to both of us."

"Oh? Like what?"

"The enforcers are moving in," Gabriel murmured. The circle of figures around us had slunk a few steps closer. My spine stiffened. I eased my hand into my backpack, and my fingers closed around a hard metal surface.

"More discussion on that note is possible, but first we need to confirm the exact nature of the magic you cast on your father and ex-fiancé," the man said.

Before he could go on, Rose dismissed him with a flick of her fingers. "No. There's nothing to discuss there, since you don't even consider what they were doing to *me* to be a crime. This is just a distraction to try to take us in without causing too much chaos. But I promise you, if I have to defend myself and my consorts, it won't be subtle. Do you really want half of Manhattan finding out that witching society exists?"

Of course. That was why they'd cleared the street. There didn't seem to be anything her Assembly hated more than the idea of regular people finding out about their secret magic. The hawkish guy's jaw had tightened. I smiled to myself even though my shoulders stayed tensed. Rose had his number, all right.

"I'd rather it didn't come to that," he said.

"So would I," Rose said. "We don't want to hurt anyone at all, even you. We'd just like to be left alone to live our lives. We aren't any threat to you if you leave us alone. Is there any chance at all of negotiating that?"

The man paused, and I could see in his expression that the answer was, *No way in hell.* Rose must have seen that too, not that she'd probably had much hope in the first place. Her left foot slid slightly behind her in the witch version of a fighting stance.

The man's fingers twitched with a gesture so quick I almost didn't catch it, and the figures around us whirled into motion.

The air sizzled with waves of magic. My pendant quivered harder against my skin. Rose flung out her arms and swiveled on her feet, throwing out her own magic to shield us, to knock our attackers down.

My hand jerked from my pack. My pulse thudded in my ears.

One, two, three of the enforcers toppled over at Rose's strike. But two more were rushing closer, the magic their hands were forming so potent it visibly glowed. Rose spun toward one, and my hand snapped up. I didn't let myself think, just pulled the trigger.

The pistol recoiled in my hand with a hitch I'd almost forgotten in the months since I'd last gone to the range for target practice. I'd never had to fire a gun in an actual fight. The shot thundered in the air, and the bullet slammed into the witch's shoulder. Blood bloomed stark red across her yellow T-shirt.

The woman cried out. The hawkish man who'd lead the group had whipped around at the sound. When he saw her wound, his face darkened. My gut clenched as he jabbed his hand toward us.

"Damon," Seth said through his teeth, but another hail of spells was already descending on us, even faster and sharper than before. Gabriel stumbled to the side, his hand jerking to his temple, and I swung around. Make them regret this. Make them back off. Make them scared of people hearing and coming to see the magic they were throwing around. I didn't care, as long as I got some of it done.

I fired off three more shots in quick succession: *bang, bang, bang*. My aim was shakier now. One bullet clipped a woman's thigh, another sent up a puff of brick dust where it dinged a shop corner, and the last—the last slammed into the chest of one of the guys waving his magic baton.

His body crumpled. My stomach flipped over with a lurch, and then our remaining attackers heaved a searing blaze of magic toward us.

Rose whirled around faster than I'd ever seen her, the air singing with her own magic, but even that wasn't fast enough. I rocked backward on my feet, little barbs of heat digging through my skull and rattling my thoughts, and Jin yelped at her other side. Rose's arms whipped out. Her feet pattered against the ground as she moved through the form of her spell, and in another instant the barbs fell away. A wash of cold swept away from her and collided with the enforcers and the hawkish man, toppling them.

Jin swore, holding his arm. I caught a glimpse of it: the sleeve of his shirt charred, the skin all down from there mottled with red blisters. An angry red mark slashed across his neck.

"Come on, come on," Rose was saying, choked and breathless. "I don't know how long they'll be out for. We've got to go."

She wove her fingers in the air over Jin's arm with a few darting circles, and the redness faded to a still painful-looking pink. He nodded sharply as if to say that was enough for now, and we all took off around the nearest corner.

"Put that away," Seth gritted out beside me.

The gun. I still had it clutched against my sweating palm. I shoved it in the pack before we came onto the next street. The witches hadn't cleared that one. Ordinary people were standing all around, many of them staring our way. How much had they seen and heard? Did it even matter now?

"You should get rid of it completely," Seth muttered as we hustled past those gaping faces to another street over. "That was the stupidest move I've seen from you yet."

"I took a couple of them down," I said.

"You pissed them off even more," he said. "Now they think *we're* dangerous too. Maybe too dangerous to even try to keep any of us alive."

He was just being the same old buzzkill Seth he always was. I told myself that, but my pulse hiccupped as I glanced at Rose.

She looked back at me, her expression tight. "I know what you meant to do. You were just trying to help protect us. It's okay."

She said that, but my stomach sank anyway, because I could hear the fear in her voice—not of me, I didn't think, but of what her Assembly might do next. As we ran on, our feet pounding the concrete, the image of the one guy falling with a bullet hole in his chest replayed in my memory.

I'd had to do it. I'd *had* to. But my gut sank even lower with each repetition.

I just had to hope I'd helped things more than hurt them.

CHAPTER THIRTEEN

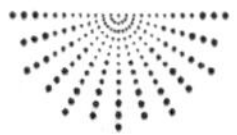

Rose

I stopped in a little courtyard between a couple of shops. We'd come several blocks, and no reaching whisper of magic had touched me yet. I didn't know how severely I'd taken down the enforcers, but they obviously weren't bouncing back quickly.

My heart was still thumping away twice as fast as normal, adrenaline singing through my veins. The lingering sweetness of blueberry jam from my breakfast had turned sour in my mouth.

The guys came to a halt around me. I immediately turned to Jin. He was holding his arm a little away from his chest—any contact must have still been painful. Sucking in my breath, I motioned him closer and studied the mottled burns that streaked down his skin from his neck to his wrist.

"They're not so bad now," he said, but the rough note

in his voice gave him away. They were hurting him even *without* any contact.

"I can do a better job of healing them," I said. "Now that we're out of the line of fire."

I worked the magic with my hands over his body, knitting together the broken flesh and cooling the sting as well as I could. Jin's shoulders had come down half an inch by the time I was finished, so I guessed I'd done an all right job.

He flexed the muscles and turned his arm one way and then the other. "Good as new," he said with a smile, even though pink marks still mottled his olive-brown skin like scars. I wasn't sure those would ever fade completely.

Imagining how much damage that spell might have done if he hadn't been wearing his protective pendant made my stomach churn.

"Is anyone else hurt?" I asked, glancing around at the other guys. In the chaos of the fight, I wasn't sure I'd been able to keep track of everyone's injuries.

I got nods all around. Gabriel cleared his throat. "I think maybe we should talk about other lines of fire." He cocked his head at Damon. "Bringing a gun to a magic fight—*maybe* something it'd have been good to discuss with the rest of us ahead of time?"

He said it in his usual calm, almost gentle way of chiding, but Damon immediately bristled. "What, so you all could have freaked out and told me to ditch it? I know I do things differently from the rest of you, but some of the things I've learned are actually useful when you've got murderous witches after you, you know. I'm probably ten times better prepared for protecting myself against anyone this vicious than any of you are."

His voice was brash, but I saw a twitch of his eyelid that made me think he wasn't as certain as he was trying to sound. Seth had already laid into him about the gun. I wasn't all that crazy about Damon going around with a weapon like that either—the crack of it firing still jittered through my nerves whenever I remembered it—but it wasn't as if he'd necessarily hurt our attackers any more than my own magic had. So, who was I to judge, exactly?

I took Damon's hand. "I meant what I said before. I'm *glad* you had it so you could help fight back. I have no idea what the Assembly people after us are going to make of it... but there's not much we can do about that now, right?"

"Yeah," he muttered. His fingers squeezed mine and then let go. There was something pained in his expression that I didn't like.

"Are you okay?" I asked.

He gave me a smile that looked a little forced. "It'll take more than those bastards to get me down, angel."

I didn't think he'd respond well to being pressed harder, especially when the other guys were already on that job.

"Can I just say I'd like to know if you picked up any more exciting items from those associates you met up with yesterday?" Kyler said with a tight grin.

"I got a few pistols," Damon said. "In case anyone decided they wanted to go into these fights armed too. So we're not leaving Rose to do all the work."

My stomach flipped right over. "Hey," I said, and

waited until he met my eyes again. "I'm not doing all the work anyway. I need you—all of you. If it wasn't for you, I'd be a miserable slave to a consort who hated me. So don't for one second think you haven't done enough."

"What do we do now?" Seth asked into the silence that followed. "They know we're in New York. Should we hit the road again?"

"Where would we go?" Gabriel said. "We'd still have the same problems. We came here because Rose thought there were people who'd help." He tipped his head to me. "Do you think we should risk meeting up with that woman from the shop?"

I inhaled and exhaled slowly, gathering my thoughts. "It's almost time for us to meet her at the park anyway. I don't think the people after us will attack us again right away—they never have before. They'll need time to decide on another plan." One of the few times the Assembly's bureaucracy had benefitted me. "You're right. We have to see if we can find people who'll help us, information we can use against them, or we'll end up losing no matter where we go. But let's hurry. If we're lucky, she'll get there early and we won't have to stick around here too long."

We flagged a couple of cabs—no way were we all squeezing into one—and I sat on the edge of my seat as the driver wove through the streets and crossed over the bridge back to Staten Island. The taxi dropped us off at the edge of the park.

A salt-laced breeze blew through the trees from the shoreline I couldn't see. A few kids were playing on the playground while their parents watched. I checked the signs and led the guys between the scattered trees to a signpost I could see in the distance near a thicker stretch of forest. That was where Margo Elands had said we should meet her.

When we were close, I motioned for the guys to stop. "I think you should let me wait for her alone. She sounded a little weirded out by the whole public meeting thing... I don't want her to get overwhelmed."

"We'll be right here if you need us, Sprout," Gabriel said. Kyler gave me a playful salute.

Leaving them behind sent a tug through my chest, even though I was only walking about twenty feet away from them. They'd be able to see me the whole time; I'd be able to look over at them. And it wasn't as if I couldn't defend myself or was likely to need to against the expert on historical witching oddities.

No, it was just that it didn't feel good acting as if they shouldn't be standing beside me. As if I were ashamed of who I'd taken as my consorts, when that wasn't true in the slightest.

"I've got your back too," Philomena said, blinking into being to stroll along beside me. She gave me a wink and twirled her sun umbrella. The last few times she'd appeared, she'd looked a little translucent. I thought maybe she'd faded a little more. It seemed rude to call attention to that, though.

"Thank you for the company," I said dryly.

"Oh, I mean it. You should see what I can do with a parasol when threatened."

I had to smile. "I believe it."

I sat down on the picnic table near the signpost to

wait. Apparently Margo had shown up early. As soon as my bottom hit the wooden boards, a stout figure with a short-sleeved cardigan pulled over a pastel flowered dress emerged from the thicker woods to join me.

"Now *there* is a witch," Phil murmured, and I couldn't argue that.

Margo Elands fit the look of a stereotypical witch so well she'd probably made every faction of the Assembly cringe at least a little. Her dress might have been in pastels, but she had a knob of a chin and a jutting pointed nose, her eyes dark and deep-set. Her coarse wavy hair was a mix of gray and white, but I could tell from a few flecks still remaining that it had once been a dark mahogany brown. I guessed from the lines on her face and the slight stiffness with which she walked that she was in her sixties and a little worse for wear.

"My mysterious anonymous friend?" she said, looking me up and down.

I hadn't given her my name or any identifying details in case the Assembly had been monitoring her. "Yes. Ms. Elands?"

She waved that name off. "Margo is fine. What can I do for you, dear? I take it this isn't just about you wanting something from the shop."

"It's not," I said. "Although—has everything been all right? When I saw the shop was closed, I couldn't help worrying."

She shrugged. "I'm starting to get a little arthritis in my joints. Sometimes it acts up enough to be a problem, and I take a couple days to rest. I don't get so many regulars at the shop that it usually disturbs anyone."

"Well, nothing suspicious about that," Philomena said. "You were worried for nothing."

A breath of relief rushed out of me. Nothing I'd done had gotten Margo into any trouble. Assuming this meeting didn't.

I resisted the urge to glance over at my guys. If she hadn't already noticed me arriving with them, it was probably better not to draw her attention to them.

Her eyes had already sharpened anyway. "What exactly did you think might have happened to me?"

"Well, I..." I rubbed my mouth. There wasn't an easy way to put this. "The best I can explain it is I've gotten into some trouble with the Assembly. Or at least part of the Assembly that's dealing out their own justice without anyone else knowing much about it. I know you've had some... issues with the more conservative members in the past?"

Margo's sturdy body had stiffened. "They didn't like some of the things I dug up and talked about from our past. That's why I'm living out here and not in Seattle the last twenty years. Can't say I miss them much. But you don't want to mess with them, young witch. I promise you, you don't."

"Vaguely foreboding," Phil said, wrinkling her nose. "Not very helpful, madam."

I didn't have any humor left after that warning. Tension wrapped around my chest. "I *don't* want to mess with them. But they seem set on messing with me. I just want them to back off. I was hoping maybe from your time there, from dealing with them, you might have some advice on how to maneuver around them, or find their weak spots, or—"

Margo was shaking her head. "I don't want to get mixed up in this," she said, taking a step back. "I didn't come out too badly from the trouble I got into. I'd like to keep what I still have."

"You don't have to do anything," I said quickly. "I wouldn't ask you to stick your neck out. After you leave the park, you can forget you ever saw me. It's just, if there's anything you could say that might help..."

A pleading note had crept into my voice. I winced inwardly at it. But Margo hesitated.

"They're not all bad, you know," she said. "I had plenty of friends in the Assembly. It just doesn't do much good when the ones who crack the whip have their heads on backward. You want them off your tail? That's all?"

I nodded. "I'd disappear from witching society, just keep to myself and stay away, if they'd let me."

She sighed. "Well, I can tell you this much: If your spark is kindled, you'd better keep your magic to yourself. They've refined the art of tracing magicking at a distance over the years. And not just that magic was worked but by who, as if you've left your signature on it. You cast a spell, and they'll know your general area. Cast a couple more, and they'll pinpoint you exactly. I'd imagine that's how they've followed you so far. You want to disappear? You keep that power under wraps."

She gave me a sharp bob of her head and turned. "Thank you!" I called after her as she hurried off. My throat had gone tight.

The enforcers could trace my magicking. Then every

spell I'd cast to build our shield, to enchant our pendants, to heal my consorts in the last few days—I'd been drawing our enemies to us every time.

Could I possibly keep us far enough ahead of them to wait them out now *without* casting a single spell?

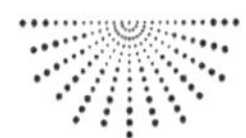

CHAPTER FOURTEEN

Rose

Gabriel pulled the SUV into the lot at the fringes of the suburban park. I peered from the window at the stretch of manicured grass and flower beds, the paths winding elegantly between the trees. A lot more upkeep went into this place than the park where I'd met Margo.

We were north of New York City proper now, among neighborhoods of huge houses with sprawling lawns and more golf courses than I could count. Closer to the kind of society I'd grown up in, but I couldn't say I felt all that comfortable.

I turned to look at Kyler, who was watching his phone in the seat behind me. "Anything?"

He shook his head. "No one in your mom's family has reached out to anyone at the Assembly since you contacted them. It's all just innocuous stuff like continuing text conversations with local friends. I don't see any indication that your aunt has told anyone else that you got in touch."

I let out my breath, wishing my nerves weren't jumping so much. Gabriel reached over and rested a reassuring hand on my arm.

"You've done everything you can to keep the Assembly off our backs," he said. "Nothing we've done should have tipped them off, right?"

"Right." As soon as I'd returned from my chat with Margo, I'd reworked the spells on our pendants so that the magic on them wouldn't activate unless I prompted it, which meant there shouldn't be anything to trace in the meantime. Then I'd magicked up a sort of illusion, a spell that would travel to the southwest, away from here, bleeding hints of magic as it went. I didn't know how long the energy I'd given it would keep it going, but for a day or two at least I could hope our enemies would think we'd left New York and follow that.

And in case they'd guessed that I might reach out to my family while I was here, we'd figured out a whole system of precautions for approaching my younger aunt, Virginia. We'd couriered her a prepaid phone Ky had hacked and installed with a tracking app, and a brief letter explaining the barest essentials of who I was and why we had to be careful communicating. She'd used that phone to set up this meeting with me.

I'd picked a park for that meeting inspired by Margo, but now all that wide open space was making me feel edgy.

"If we see any reason at all to worry, we'll alert you," Seth said.

I nodded, patting my own prepaid phone in my pocket. But if an attack came too fast, I wouldn't have time to activate their protective pendants. The inherent magic on our consort bonds would protect them a little—and I could send more power through that in an instant—but I couldn't rely on their next attack being a mild one. And that connection didn't help Gabriel at all.

I lay my hand over Gabriel's for a moment. Then I got up and leaned between the seats, reaching to the other guys. Jin and Damon moved forward from the back seat so all four of them could clasp hands with me in turn. I didn't need any magic to feel the hum of affection in the car.

"You need us, you shout," Damon said.

"And you'll be there, guns blazing?" I teased.

His expression tensed a little even at my light tone. The altercation yesterday morning was still bothering him. Maybe I'd have a chance to talk to him alone about it later, if he let me.

"She's almost here," Ky announced. He was following the signal from my aunt's phone via his app.

"Okay. I'd better go. I'll be back soon."

I shot them all one last nervous smile and headed out. The door shut behind me with a thud.

Outside, the sky was clear but the air more crisp than yesterday. It had just enough of a cool edge to sharpen my senses as I ambled down one of the paths to the small wooden gazebo where Virginia and I had agreed to meet.

The rumble of a car engine pulling into the lot

reached my ears just as I climbed the steps. I sat down on one of the benches inside and forced my hands not to fidget.

It wasn't just the Assembly I was nervous about. I was going to meet one of my mom's sisters for the first time I could remember, maybe the first time ever. I still didn't know how much they'd shut us out of their lives and how much it'd been my dad's doing. What was she going to make of me and this whole crazy situation?

Maybe she'd take off like Margo had as soon as she realized just how far in over my head I was. I couldn't even blame her if she did. We might be family by blood, but in every other way we were strangers. She didn't owe me anything, not really.

I just had to hope that blood and long-ago memories would be enough to offset the danger I might be putting her and the rest of the family in. If the Levesques couldn't help us... I had no idea who else we could turn to.

Footsteps rasped along the path. I stood up and turned to face her.

The tall slim woman approaching the gazebo had her black hair woven into a braid that formed a loose loop at the back of her head. The breeze fluttered through her airy silk dress, making the watercolor print of lilies on a pond seem to come alive. She came to a stop at the base of the steps, and for several seconds we just stared at each other.

Virginia looked like an older but softer version of my mother—at least, what I knew of my mother from the few photos I had of her. A sudden ache filled my heart at the thought of the framed photograph in my bedroom back in the home I wasn't sure I could ever return to.

Smile lines framed my aunt's eyes, and her chin and nose were more rounded than Mom's sharp features, which I'd mostly inherited. Her eyes were a lighter green. But I could see our family line written in her face so clearly I'd have recognized her even if we'd simply happened to pass each other on the street.

I guessed similar thoughts were racing through her head, because when she opened her mouth, the first thing she said was, "By the Spark, you are your mother's daughter, aren't you. It's like going back in time twenty years."

My throat choked up a little. I pushed myself to my feet. "Aunt Virginia?"

A smile dawned on her face. "Ginny," she said. "That's what Alora—your mother—always called me. What pretty much everyone in the family calls me. And you're obviously Rose."

I didn't know what to do with myself—with my hands, with my mouth. I stepped back to give Ginny room to come up the stairs. She sat down across from me, so I sat back down too, my pulse jittering.

"I'm sorry to drop into your life out of nowhere, and all the subterfuge—I didn't want to create any trouble for you," I said.

Ginny shook her head. "It's fine. It's— I've felt guilty for a long time that we weren't able to find a better way to reach out to you, after Lora... My parents had a lot of suspicions about her death, you know. Whether the illness was completely natural. They'd already raised concerns about the speed of the consorting and marriage. When the Assembly ruled against them your father was able to file a no-contact order. None of us were to try to get in touch with him or you."

So Dad had lied about that too. The lump in my throat hardened. He'd told me my whole life that my mother's family had wanted nothing to do with us, when he'd forced them to stay away.

"I had no idea," I said. "I mean, he told me that your family hadn't approved of the marriage, but he made it sound as if you'd shut us out, not the other way around."

"Well, of course. Why would he have wanted to admit why he'd done it?"

"Am I going to get you in trouble with the Assembly just by being here?" I asked. "I'm making you violate that order."

She shrugged, her smile turning wry. "If they find out, I can always say in my defense that you came to me. But you seem to be going to a lot of work to make sure they don't find out. What's going on, Rose? What kind of trouble are you in?"

It was such a long story, and so much of it I wasn't sure I could trust her or the rest of the family with yet. They might have wanted to be a part of my life, but I had no idea how they'd feel about the idea of taking an unsparked man as a consort, or taking multiple consorts, let alone both. They might decide I was some kind of deviant, corrupted by my father somehow, and send me back to the Assembly. So I had to tread carefully.

The root of it all, at least, didn't reflect on me in any unpleasant ways. "It's—it's complicated. And telling you the whole thing might put you in danger, just knowing it. You shouldn't tell anyone else, not even in the family, not yet. And I won't tell you at all if you don't want to take the risk. I'd totally understand—"

Aunt Ginny held up her hand to stop me. "I've spent more than twenty years holding my tongue and pretending I didn't have a niece out there to avoid the Assembly coming down on me. I think it's about time I stuck my neck out, now that you've come all this way."

She said it so plainly and firmly that a little of the hesitation in me melted away.

"I was supposed to be consorted," I said. "Just this month. But I found out that my father had made an arrangement with my consort-to-be that the ceremony would be distorted so that I wouldn't be able to use my magic without his permission, and I'd *have* to use it if he ordered me to." It was simpler not to mention my stepmother's role in the whole thing, now that she was gone anyway.

Ginny's face had turned sallow. "That's *awful*."

I twisted my hands together in my lap. "I... took measures to make sure that didn't happen. But it turns out that Dad had backing from some faction in the Assembly. They want to prosecute me for what I did to defend myself, and they'd let him and my former fiancé get off free. I swear to you, I didn't hurt anyone, or do anything that puts the witching community in danger. But they want to cover up what happened, I guess, and their own involvement. I've only uncovered a little, but it sounds like there are other witches they've trapped in similar ways."

"Your mother," my aunt said, her voice a little ragged. "We hadn't heard from her in over a year. We thought your father had completely convinced her that we were the enemy, trying to tear them apart. But then I got this letter saying something about how he wanted to take her power... It didn't really make sense, and it was from when she was sick. Our parents used it as evidence after she died, but the Assembly's court dismissed it as hallucination. Maybe it wasn't, though."

To take her power. How could Dad have done that back then? His messages with Frankford had indicated that the binding he'd had my stepmother work out was a new strategy they hadn't tried before. What had they used to manipulate witches in the past? And had they really been doing it for that long?

What *for*? Celestine had said they wanted to control me because of how much power I'd had. Both the Hallowell line and the Levesque's were strong magically, and the two combined... I'd seen for myself now how much power I could wield already. But Dad couldn't have used that excuse with my mother. What would he have done with her magic—what *had* he done? Had the Assembly known even then?

All those unanswerable questions condensed in my stomach, leaving me queasy. Ginny leaned across the gazebo and gripped my hand. "They can't keep getting away with this. We can't let them. Anything I can do to keep you safe, you just let me know."

Tears burned in the back of my eyes. I wanted so badly to trust her, to spill the whole story and be wrapped up in the protection of a family who really would have my back. But it wasn't just me who needed safety. And she wasn't the only one on her side of the equation either. There were too many factors for me to risk diving in headfirst.

"Thank you," I said. "I'm still figuring out where to go from here. Can you give me a little time to think about what I'd need? And then I'll reach out to you again."

"Of course," Ginny said. "Take whatever time you need. Just don't hesitate if you think of anything."

I held her gaze intently for a moment. "And can you promise you won't mention me or anything I told you to anyone else in the family, just for now? The more people know, the more likely the wrong people could find out I'm here..."

"Of course. Of course. Don't you worry about that for a second."

She got up, and I stood too. The second I was on my feet, she opened her arms, offering a hug without pushing it on me. I blinked hard and stepped into her embrace. Just for an instant, it felt almost as if I'd found my mother again.

"I'll be back in touch soon," I said. "Thank you again, so much. It means a lot just knowing I have someone here."

Now I just had to wait to make sure I really had her on my side—that her words hadn't been as false as so many of my dad's had been.

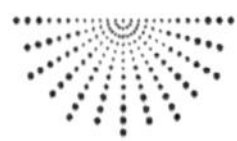

CHAPTER FIFTEEN

Gabriel

I lay back on the lumpy hotel-room bed, my thumb skimming over the screen of the cheap tablet Kyler had picked up for each of us on his last expedition into the tech stores. "Might as well be able to use the internet when it's available for free," he'd said cheerfully as he'd handed them out. "Just don't sign into any of your pre-existing accounts, and no one will be the wiser."

Ky was sitting on the room's other bed, hunched over the full laptop he'd bought himself. The keys clattered under his speedy fingers. There wasn't much in the room except us, the beds, and a carpet that gave off a slightly mildewy smell into the air. A pretty far cry from the gleaming apartment Jin's friend had lent him, but at least there was no reason for the Assembly goons to check some rinky-dink hotel just far enough from Newark airport that no one really wanted to stay here.

"Still looking good?" I asked Ky.

He nodded, his eyes never leaving the screen. "I've been watching all the phone lines, their internet service—everything I can get access to. No one in the Levesque family has given any indication they even know Rose exists. Either her aunt is keeping the secret as promised, or anyone else she's told knows better than to spread the word."

"How long do you think we should give them before Rose reaches out again?"

Ky rubbed his hand over his face. "I don't know. It's always going to be a crapshoot to some extent. But everything she said about the meet-up sounded positive."

"So you're leaning toward trusting them."

"Well..." He grinned at me. "I'm leaning toward giving them at least a little more rope to see whether they hang themselves with *that*, at the very least."

"We can't be too cautious," I pointed out. "If we can trust them, we're going to need them sooner, not later." Staying in this motel in Newark worked for now, but I couldn't imagine how it was sustainable. I'd seen how dogged our attackers were. At some point Rose was going to have to cast magic again, and then they'd be on us—unless we had a better way of stopping them.

"True, true." Ky sighed. "Now, if I had ears right inside their houses... But that might be a little extreme even for me." He laughed a little to himself, and I made a mental note to always stay on Kyler Lennox's good side.

I turned back to my own way of contributing

something, which was looking through the odd job postings on a website I'd used before to find bits of work here and there while I'd been traveling. Most of the offerings were pretty menial, but every now and then a listing popped up from someone willing to trust a relative stranger with their car. I could go in, give an engine a onceover, and have it running properly again in less than an hour most times. And that paid a hell of a lot better than carting someone's moving boxes around.

The money we had on us wasn't infinitely sustainable either. Might as well get a head start on restocking our funds.

There weren't any quick and easy jobs on offer today, though. I grimaced at the tablet and set it down. The one problem with being under a sort of lockdown was I did get a little stir-crazy when I couldn't roam around. Rose and the other guys were in their own rooms down the hall. We'd come in one pair at a time and asked for separate rooms, in case the Assembly started checking around for large groups with only one woman. But even if she wasn't right here with me, I didn't want to leave the motel without her either.

The Assembly had hit us too many times, too hard, for me to feel comfortable even with the few walls between us right now.

It was still an hour before we were supposed to meet up to grab dinner. What else could I do with the time that might be useful? I'd already spent a couple hours checking over the SUV this afternoon, repairing a few bits and pieces that hadn't come out of the crash unscathed, stashing some more stores of gas in the back.

I'd even managed to fix the windows, thanks to some replacement glass I'd grabbed at an auto shop on our way to the hotel. It was ready to go if we needed to make a run that way, at least.

I brought up a map of the area to consider escape routes by road. A thump sounded on the other side of the wall next to my bed. Then a moan filtered through, low and needy.

Ky glanced over and chuckled. "Glad someone's having a good time."

It wasn't Rose. Her room and the other guys' was in the opposite direction, with a couple between theirs and ours. But hearing two strangers go at it made me think of her anyway, with a tightness in my groin.

I wanted her, so badly. I could *have* her now. But I had to think about what was best for all of us. She had four consorts who could not only light her up with pleasure but with magic too. It only made sense for me to step back for the time being and wait on the sidelines until she didn't need that energy quite so much.

Another moan carried through the wall. I rolled my eyes and got up to use the bathroom—and maybe relieve some pressure in a different way.

I'd only made it halfway across the room when a now familiar pain smacked me across the head.

The wave of magic cut through my senses and jabbed down my spine. I closed my eyes and gritted my teeth against it, my feet stumbling to a stop. The Assembly's enforcers hadn't thrown anything at us since that last skirmish when Damon had brought out his gun. I'd started to think they might have quit that strategy.

No such luck.

Kyler had sucked in his breath with a hitch. A moment later, his shoulders came down as Rose must have sent more magic through their consort bond. She'd said she didn't think they could trace that because the connection was already established. The pain in my own head eased, but it couldn't have been because of her.

No, it wasn't going away. It was just shifting. An eerie sensation wriggled through my nerves. I found myself turning toward the door. Just to get out, just to stretch my legs. I'd wanted to get some air, hadn't I?

My heart hiccupped. That wasn't my impulse. The magic was propelling me somehow.

"Where are you going?" Kyler said.

"I—" The sensation wrapped around my throat, making it harder to speak. I forced the words out. "Their magic is pushing me."

I tried to fight it, tensing against the movements. My steps dragged, but my feet still edged toward the door. Ky's eyes widened.

"I'll tell Rose," he said, grabbing his phone. "She can help block them."

"No!" I wrenched out. "I can shut this down. I just need time. If she has to cast an actual spell, that'll bring them right here. That's what they want."

That might even be why they were doing it in the first place. Trying to provoke her into using magic that would reveal where we were. I couldn't let that happen.

"Gabriel—"

"Don't you dare," I gritted out. "I'm going to see where this is taking me, and maybe it'll wear off in another minute or two. And if it doesn't, I'll figure out how to break it."

Ky hesitated and then scrambled off the bed. "Fine. I won't get her involved yet. But I'm coming with you."

I couldn't exactly stop him. I couldn't even stop myself. I gave in to the urge for a moment to give myself a chance to gather strength and consider my options. My hand rose to the door knob and opened it. I ambled out into the hall, Ky right behind me.

I half-expected my legs to carry me toward Rose's room, but of course that wouldn't make sense. Whoever was sending this magic at us didn't know where she was. So where did they want me to go? Were they going to try to walk me across the country to wherever that magical decoy of hers had led them to?

The impulse told me to get out of the building. I moved toward the elevators. With each step I tested how difficult it would be to change direction, to stop completely. Every time I tried to exert control over my muscles, the magic shoved me harder.

Shit. I couldn't let them ruin this brief respite we'd found. We weren't ready to face them again.

Kyler obviously wasn't affected at all anymore. Whatever power Rose was able to channel through their consort bond had shielded him completely now. He watched me, his expression worried, as he kept pace with me to the elevators.

"Are you sure—"

"Yes," I snapped, the lack of control fraying my temper. "I'll tell you if I need help. Maybe—maybe if you just distract me from the impulse. Talk about something that'll get my thoughts going in a different direction." Maybe then I'd be able to break this hold.

"A different direction," Ky murmured to himself as the elevator arrived. Thankfully it was empty. I automatically reached for the button that would take us to the lobby.

"Rose," he said. "You want to talk about her? She's plenty distracting." He grinned a little tightly, his gaze still anxious as it lingered on my face. "Do you remember that time when we were kids and someone had the bright idea of going to the apple orchard after that thunderstorm? The whole place was a mud slick. We practically skated on the stuff—until we'd all fallen down at least ten times and there was as much mud on us as the ground."

I did remember: the earthy, gritty flavor that had worked itself even into my mouth, the giggles carrying between the trees, Rose's dark green eyes lit with a brilliant light amid the dirt streaked all over her face. Her amusement had faltered for a few minutes when she'd thought about going back in the house looking like that, but the weather had come to rescue us, dumping another heaving of cool rain all over us and washing us clean.

I tried to focus on that impression of water rushing over my skin, as if it could carry away the magic compelling me now. Resistance shivered through my muscles. The elevator dinged as it reached its destination.

My legs balked—but only for a couple seconds. Then, with an ache that spread up from my knees, they jerked forward.

I looked up at the glass doors that separated the

elevator alcove from the main lobby, and a new urge tickled up my throat. I clamped my lips tight against it, but it didn't leave.

Oh, no. Understanding hit me. They weren't going to make me come all the way to them. They just wanted me in a public enough place where I could shout and make a scene, do who knew what crazy things, so they'd hear about it.

Panic flashed through my body. My fingers closed around the door handle. I clenched my jaw. I let my arm push the door open, and then I gripped the door frame and yanked the handle back with every shred of control I could summon.

The door slammed back into the frame—and into my other hand. Pain splintered through my nerves. I gasped with it, staggering.

"Gabriel!"

A couple people in the lobby had turned to look. I propelled myself back toward the elevators, pain still radiating up my arm in pulsing shards. A metallic taste trickled through my mouth—I'd bitten my tongue.

But I came to a stop at the elevators without being driven back. The outside impulses had faded. I'd managed to sever that magical hold after all.

Ky had lifted his phone. I grabbed his wrist with my good hand.

"No," I rasped. "I'm okay now. I stopped it. See? We can go back to the room now."

He gazed at me for a long moment before he lowered his arm. "You're sure?"

"I'm sure." I held up the hand I'd bashed. It was

already red with burst blood vessels under the skin. Fuck, it hurt, but I'd never welcomed pain more. "I showed them they can't use me like a puppet."

We got back on the elevator, and I sagged back against the wall. My body felt as exhausted as if the magic had wrung me out like a towel. Ky shifted his weight from foot to foot beside me as the elevator ascended.

"That impulse to come down here—it only grabbed *you*," he said, and then his expression shuttered. "Oh."

"Because I've got no consort bond," I said. My gut twisted. And that very fact made me a total liability. What if next time they hit us even harder? What if I didn't find a way to throw their spell off?

I rubbed my hand, wincing at its throbbing, but a deeper discomfort filled my chest. I'd tried to keep it from Rose—how much more I was struggling with the attacks than the other guys. I hadn't wanted to add even more stress to her life right now. But she needed to know.

There wasn't any getting around it. Either I formed that bond with her, or she'd be safer if I was a million miles away.

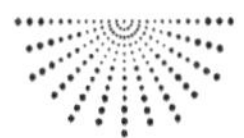

CHAPTER SIXTEEN

Rose

For just a little while, eating dinner in a burger place down the street from our hotel with the five guys I loved with all my heart, life felt almost normal. Almost *good*.

"That's not a burger," Damon informed Jin, eyeing the other guy's tofu-and-goat-cheese combo. "*This* is a burger." He hefted his half-pounder stuffed with pickles, cheese, and bacon.

"Are you going vegetarian on us?" Kyler teased.

"I had beef with lunch," Jin said with a smile. "I believe in variety. Like certain other people I'm fond of." He shot a wink at me. He hadn't said it loud enough for anyone around us to hear, even if they'd have guessed what he meant, but I blushed anyway.

"I still say it's not really a burger unless there's a cow

in it." Damon elbowed Seth, who'd ended up in the booth beside him. "Someone's got to back me up here."

Seth gave him a dubious look. "And you think it's going to be me?" Then he shook his head with a brief chuckle. "I think I'll just worry about what I want to eat." He dug into his own burger.

"Hear, hear," Gabriel said with a slanted grin. He chomped on one of his French fries.

"And my chicken burger is very good, thank you very much," I said to Damon.

He gave me a light tap with his foot under the table. "I guess I'll forgive you a few sins."

I sipped my cola and leaned against the padded back of the booth. The air smelled like salt and grease, and some sappy country song from decades ago was playing on the crackly speakers. I hadn't eaten in a place like this in, well, a long time. Maybe once or twice in Portland when I'd been off on rambles on my own, but sitting tucked away in some corner alone was nothing like this. I could believe I belonged here, in regular unsparked society with my unsparked men. Just leave all of the witching world behind.

If only they'd let me go.

I didn't want to think about that right at this moment. I took another bite of my burger, savory chicken and mayo and doughy bun mixing together in my mouth, and tried to soak up as much of this normal, happy atmosphere as I could.

It might have been easier if I hadn't noticed early on that Gabriel seemed a little quieter than usual. He was still present, laughing at the others' jokes and directing the conversation when something struck him, but in the moments in between, when he paused to take a breath, his smile dipped a little. A hint of a shadow touched his bright blue eyes.

Well, why wouldn't he be worried? It wasn't as if I could completely shake off all thought of our precarious situation either. That's what I told myself, anyway.

The waitress came to clear our plates with a flash of a smile and a cock of her head. "Always nice seeing a bunch of friends enjoying themselves." She raised an eyebrow at me. "Don't leave 'em hanging too long before you pick one, honey. Have a lovely night!"

We managed to contain our laughter until she'd walked away to get the bill. Then sputters carried all around the table.

"All right, Briar Rose," Jin said, slinging his arm around my shoulders. "Who are you going to choose?"

Damon grinned darkly. "Maybe we should demonstrate just how good we are at sharing."

"No!" I said, pointing a finger at him. "Don't you dare start anything like that. We're *supposed* to look like we're just a bunch of friends, remember?"

Ky's eyes glinted with mischief. "Anyway, clearly if Rose were going to pick anyone, it'd be me. Brains over brawn, right?"

I squeezed Jin's hand and tipped my head just briefly against Seth's shoulder at my other side. "I think I'm happy taking both, thank you."

As we walked back to the motel, Gabriel fell into step beside me. He took my hand, twining his fingers around mine. His touch could still provoke a flutter in my chest.

But his low voice and the words he said turned it into an anxious quiver.

"I need to talk to you about something when we get back."

I glanced up at him. "What? Did something happen?" I'd felt a probing wave of magic wash through the city earlier this afternoon, but Gabriel had acted as if it hadn't affected him that much.

"You could say that. But it can wait until we've got some privacy."

In the dim hall outside our rooms, Seth paused by the one he and I had ended up sharing and took in Gabriel's and my joined hands. He dipped his head in acknowledgment. "I'll keep Ky company?" he said.

Gabriel offered him a crooked smile that looked more like his usual easy and confident self. "You can have her back for the night."

"Hey, take as long as you want. Rose belongs to herself, not any of us." Seth gave us a little salute and followed the others to the farther rooms.

I swiped the keycard and turned toward Gabriel as the door thumped shut behind us. "Now will you tell me what's going on?"

He moved closer to me, setting a hand on my waist. With a nudge, he walked me back a step so I could lean against the wall. His other hand came up to brush my cheek. He gazed into my eyes for several seconds, so intently I didn't know what to say.

My breath caught when he dipped his head toward mine. He caught my mouth with a kiss so soft and sweet the fluttering in my chest came back at full force. My fingers curled into the soft waves at the nape of his neck as I kissed him back, reveling in the moment. But I couldn't lose myself completely. I knew Gabriel well enough not to believe he'd asked me in here just for this.

His lips slid from mine to kiss my cheek. "I love you," he said. "You know that, don't you?"

My heart squeezed. "I didn't think you'd be here if you didn't," I said, but the teasing comment fell flat. I tipped my face against his shoulder. "I love you too."

His arms came around me. For a minute, he just held me, and I melted into his warmth. Still waiting. His hand stroked over my hair. Then he drew back to look at me properly.

"That's why I'm here," he said. "And that's why I'm not sure I should be. Not like this, not anymore."

My brow furrowed. "What are you talking about?"

"When that attack hit this afternoon..." His jaw tensed. "They compelled me with magic. Tried to force me to go outside and make some kind of scene to help them figure out where we are."

Moldy cinders. No wonder he was upset. "But you didn't," I said. "You stopped them."

He held up his right hand, the one that had been resting on my waist. A dark bruise mottled the whole back of it. I sucked in my breath in horrified shock. He was left-handed, so I hadn't noticed anything odd about him mostly using that one during dinner—he must have managed to keep the bruise out of view without me realizing.

"This is how I stopped them," he said. "That's what it took. I couldn't shake them otherwise. And next time, if they're closer or they just try harder, I might not be able to do it at all."

"If I'd known—"

"You would've used your magic to ward them off," he filled in for me. "I know. That's why I didn't tell you. Because then they still would have figured out where we are, so how would that have helped anything?"

"I can't let them hurt you—or make you hurt yourself," I protested.

"I know." He lowered his head again. His voice roughened. "The way I see it, there's only two ways this can work so that I'm not a danger to you. Either I become your consort, so I have the same bond you can use to protect me like you do for the other guys, or I leave and hide out somewhere else where it won't matter if I give myself away."

"No," I said firmly, shaking my head. "No. At this point, I don't think they'd just let you go. You've seen way too much. They'd probably find you anyway, and the Spark only knows what they'd do to you if they caught you alone." I paused, touching his face to bring his gaze back to mine. "I mean, unless you'd rather take your chances that way."

"I wouldn't," he said. "I'm in this, Rose. I've been in this since the moment I got back, even if it took me a long time to admit just how much I wanted you. I want to *be* with you, every way I can. I'd have gone into the ceremony that day at Seth's house if you'd let me. Are *you* ready?"

I swallowed hard. "I don't want you binding yourself to me because you feel like you have to."

His laugh came out hoarse. "It's not like that. Not even slightly. I know you, and I know what I want. There's no one in this world I'd want to commit myself to other than you. Unless... unless there's some other reason you don't want to go through with it."

My pulse lurched. "No. No, it's not—" I didn't know how to put the feeling swelling inside me into words. I tugged him to me and kissed him hard, as if that heat between us could say enough on its own.

Five consorts. Five men who would act as my husbands and more. From the moment Gabriel had walked back into my life, that thought had been there in my head. I'd wanted it before I'd even been sure he felt the same way.

"There isn't anything I'd like more," I said when we eased apart. "I just wish... it could have happened differently."

"Me too. But you trust me, don't you? To know I'm ready, no matter what else is going on."

When he put it that way, yeah, I did. If any of us had always known their own mind, it was Gabriel. The corners of my lips curled up, but my smile was bittersweet. "Okay. But I don't even know if the consort ceremony will work when I'm already consorted. The other guys, we kind of did it all at once. And I don't know how we can do it without *that* magic bringing the Assembly down on us."

"Yeah." He was silent for a moment. "Isn't there anything that can shield your magic, make it so they wouldn't be able to detect it, even for a little while?"

"Not that I know of," I said. "Nothing except more

magic, I suppose. And of course if I cast some kind of shielding spell to mask it, the shielding spell will tip them off. If we had another witch who could cast a shield, someone they don't see as a criminal..."

Oh. My fingers grasped his shirt where they'd been resting on his chest.

"What?" he said.

"My aunts," I said. "Ky thinks Ginny is keeping my secret—the part she knows, anyway—right? If we wait until tomorrow, give it a whole day and there's still no sign that we need to worry, maybe it's time I tell her the whole story. See if she could shelter us, at least for long enough for us to do the ceremony."

"Would that work?" Gabriel asked. "Her shielding it?"

"I think so. Any witch should be able to mask my magic. And the Levesques are a powerful family." I drew in my breath with a shiver of nervous anticipation. "I'm going to have to trust someone sometime. We can't keep running on our own."

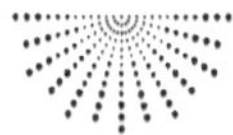

CHAPTER SEVENTEEN

Rose

My house back home on the Hallowell estate had always felt like a castle, all that old stone and the turrets rising from its walls. The main building on the younger Levesque estate was more of a proper country home, with a sweeping covered porch around its robin's egg blue body and big airy rooms boasting huge windows and pale hardwood floors. The furniture was all in muted earthy tones, and the smell of hay and fresh mown grass drifted through those windows, stirred by the ceiling fans overhead.

"Both my husband—Owen—and I had older sisters," Aunt Ginny had told us when she'd escorted us inside. "So neither of us had an estate to inherit. Instead, we've built a new one of our own. I think it's turned out rather well."

Not that we'd spent much time talking about her

house. No, the morning had been dedicated to explaining my rather unusual situation first to her in another park meeting, and then, when she didn't recoil in revulsion, coming here to lay it all out for the rest of the younger branch of my mother's family. My aunt, reasonably, hadn't thought it fair to offer her property to harbor theoretical criminals and theoretically criminal magic without running it by the rest of the relatives.

So now the five guys and I were sitting on linen couches in the house's bright living room while Ginny's husband, her two daughters, and the older daughter's husband took in our story. I'd asked the guys to let me do most of the talking, and I didn't think they'd minded. It was intimidating enough for me to be explaining this to four members of witching society who all looked as though their eyes were ready to fall out of their heads.

"There is a precedent," I said, my hands clenched together on my lap. "At least, I think there is, for having multiple consorts. I've seen etchings on an old witching building on the Hallowell property showing it, and a witching historian confirmed she's seen them elsewhere, but that the Assembly goes out of their way to destroy that evidence."

The older daughter, Naomi, laughed a little breathlessly and glanced at her husband, Greg. "Can you imagine?" she said with a playful glint in her light brown eyes and a swish of her chestnut ponytail. "Maybe I should add a couple more to my entourage."

From Greg's grimace, I didn't think he liked the idea of sharing his wife and consort at all, but he managed to answer in a similarly teasing tone. "I don't think you'd ever win the cover-stealing contest if there were three of us to contend with."

"Hmm. That would be a concern." She turned back to me, her expression still amused. From what I'd gathered, Naomi was a couple years younger than me and only recently married. She didn't seem fazed by my unusual consorting at all.

Owen, Aunt Ginny's husband, looked more perplexed than anything. "And your spark is kindled?" he said. "Even though none of them is from a witching line? Are you sure there isn't any witching blood in your families?" His gaze skimmed over the guys on either side of me.

"It is kindled," I said before they felt any pressure to try to answer on their own. "And I suppose it's possible one or two of them might, farther back, but I can't believe *all* of them do. It would be too huge a coincidence. My spark reacts to all of them. But that's not the point. This faction of the Assembly doesn't approve of our consorting either way."

"I don't understand," the younger daughter, Stella, spoke up. Like Naomi, she'd inherited her father's chestnut-brown hair, but her eyes were green like her mother's. Her waves had been cut at an ear-length bob that made her thin face look even narrower. She was only nineteen, not yet consorted or close to it. "Why should it matter to them? If your spark is kindled, it's kindled. If your consorts accept witching society, why shouldn't witching society accept them?"

"Very good questions," Jin said with a smile, leaning back against the couch.

My uncle Owen gave him a wary look. "We've kept to our own for good reasons. Witches and the unsparked don't have the most pleasant history of mixing." He turned to me again. "I can't blame you for the decisions you made. The pressure you were under, the threat you were facing—but taking this route would be hard even if the Assembly wasn't interfering. Your consorts have ties to the unsparked world. How many people will know about your magic by the end of this? How are *their* people going to react to this relationship?"

"We're not going to go sharing Rose's secrets with the rest of the world," Damon said. "Give us a little credit. And who and how I hook up with anyone is none of anyone else's business."

Seth and Kyler exchanged a look. "We wouldn't talk about the magical side of things around anyone else either," Seth said. "Our parents, well... Like Damon says, they don't need to know those details."

"I don't have anyone to hassle me," Gabriel said. "But it is a small town. I see your point. People will notice something. They'll gossip. But we can deal with that when it comes to it. We're never going to come to it if the Assembly keeps attacking us and Rose."

"You *did* cast illegal magic," Greg said to me.

My chest tightened. "I did. But only what I had to in order to save myself. I'll gladly face prosecution for that —*if* the crimes committed against me are also recognized and given due weight. And if they leave my consorts out of it. The guys have never hurt anyone at all."

Damon shifted beside me at that, and the echo of gunshots passed through my mind. Well, that was one more thing we'd deal with when we came to it, if we ever got to.

Aunt Ginny was shaking her head with a wry smile. "I can't imagine what your mother would have made of all this. But I think she'd have been proud that you found your way out of that trap your father set for you, no matter how. She'd be proud that you followed your heart. I can see how much you care about all of them—and how much they care about you. So..." She threw her hands in the air. "I say, who are we to judge?"

Naomi cocked her head, her gaze turning a little more serious. "It's not just about judgment, though, is it? You wouldn't have come to us and told us all this unless you needed something."

A flush crept over my cheeks. "I would have wanted to reach out anyway. It's only that I wouldn't have taken the risk right now if our situation wasn't so dire."

"Oh, that's absolutely what I meant," she said, waving off my embarrassment. "Not intended as a criticism. Just a question."

I took a slow breath. Somehow this part was harder than laying out all the rest. "Gabriel and I reconnected later. He wasn't there when we did the first consorting ceremony. But we're just as much in love, just as willing to commit to each other. He's one of us. And the Assembly's efforts are hurting him so much more than the others because it's so much harder for me to protect him. I want to see if I can complete the ceremony with him as well. And since they're tracking my magic, I'd need to do that somewhere other magic can hide what I'm doing."

"You want to conduct the consorting ceremony here," Owen said. I couldn't read his tone.

"We could do it tonight," I said quickly. "I've conducted it on my own before—I wouldn't need anyone to get directly involved. It'd just take some magicking to cover up what I'm doing. We'd leave in the morning if that's all you'd want to do with us. I don't want to bring the Assembly down on you. I just... It's the only way I can see us surviving more than another few days. And I didn't have anyone else to turn to."

"This is what you want?" Ginny said to Gabriel. "You know what a commitment the consorting bond is."

"I know," he said steadily. "I know my life might be a lot easier if I went back to living it the way I was before. But it'd also be a whole lot emptier. I'll take that trade, without hesitation."

"And the rest of you don't mind having a little more competition for my cousin's affections?" Naomi asked with an arch of her eyebrows.

Jin laughed. "It's not competition. It's more hands on deck." He grinned so slyly my blush deepened into a burn.

"It probably sounds strange," Ky put in, leaning forward. "It would to me if I wasn't part of it. But we spent six years together when we were growing up, being there for each other, having each other's backs... I've never been as close with anyone as with the five people around me here, and that includes everyone, not just Rose."

"It feels right," Seth added when his twin paused. "We're just better when we're together."

"Yeah," Damon said, his voice low. "We are."

Ginny looked to her husband. "Do we need to discuss this on our own?"

He took her hand, and even though there was still some skepticism in his expression, his affection for her shone on his face. A little of the tension in me relaxed.

"You want to say yes," he said, an observation rather than a question.

She nodded. "There's a small chance the Assembly will find out and accuse us of who knows what? Oh well. We *should* have pushed harder back when Alora first ran off with Maxim, or when she died, or... any time since then. If we had, maybe Rose wouldn't have been backed into a corner like this to begin with. If we don't stand up to them at all... What if some suitor tried to arrange a consorting like that for Stella?"

My younger cousin paled. "Okay. That's it. I'm just not getting married."

"Hey." Naomi nudged her sister. "We're not letting any creeps get their paws on you or your magic." Her gaze slid back to me. "I'm in. I say we do this. Not just for tonight—I think you should be able to stay here until we figure out how to get this faction of the Assembly off your back."

Ginny was still watching Owen's reaction. He rubbed his square jaw. Then he nodded to her and to me.

"Let's see how tonight goes. You do your ceremony. We can play it by ear from there."

CHAPTER EIGHTEEN

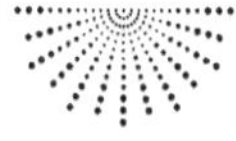

Jin

$\mathcal{I}$ could hear Rose talking with her cousin before I reached the "magicking room" they'd ducked into. "I suppose this bowl would work—oh, no, wait, this one is better. You have charcoal sticks?"

"Right here," Naomi's amused voice said in return.

The supplies rustled. Rose laughed to herself, but the sound was a little strained. "I only need two this time. Have to remember that."

"Yeah, I guess it must have been quite the ceremony the first time. Four all at once! Mine was intense enough with just one consort."

A jolt of heat shot to my cock just at one flash of memory from that night. Rose's voice dipped with a shy but also sly note that warmed me even more. "Yeah. It was pretty amazing, all right."

I came to a stop by the doorway and leaned against the frame. The two women looked over at me, Rose's usual welcoming smile a little tired around the edges, Naomi's filled with mischief. The way they were standing together, you could almost believe they'd grown up together as close cousins rather than just having met earlier today.

"Anything I can help with?" I asked, peering into the room. A wide wooden cabinet filled one wall. Otherwise the place was spartan. It reminded me a little of an artist's studio, just a very neat one with the only natural light coming from a skylight in the ceiling.

Rose swept her fingers through her hair, scattering it over her shoulders. "I don't know. I think we've got just about everything for the ceremony now. What else did we— The ribbons. I don't have them. I'll need two lengths of rope or twine."

"Right on it!" Naomi said brightly. She rummaged in the cupboard. "Any preference of color."

"Blue," I said automatically. "For one. The other one white."

Rose's eyes darted to me, but it shouldn't surprise her that I'd noticed. We'd given her those ribbons as a gift back when we were kids, right before she'd been torn away from us, six in different colors. She'd used five of them, one for herself and one for each of us, in the original consorting ceremony. Of course I'd seen which one she'd kept in reserve.

She'd used white for herself. The purple one for me, which seemed a reasonable choice—vibrant, a little decadent. Red for Damon and his passionate temper.

Green for Seth's supportive strength. Yellow for Kyler's bright intellect.

Blue fit Gabriel perfectly. The guy had the same steady, persuasive pull as an ocean tide. My fingers itched. When we got back home—because we were going to, that was the only answer I'd accept—I should make a painting of our group. All our colors woven together like we'd once woven those ribbons, only with all the new complexities now that we'd grown up.

"Blue and white it is." There was a click of scissors, and then another, and Naomi handed Rose two lengths of cord about as long as her forearm. Rose set them in the bowl with the other supplies she'd collected.

"You're happy with the dress you picked out?" Naomi asked. "If you want to take another look through my things..."

"It's fine," Rose said, smiling at her. "It's perfect. I just need something simple that I can move in."

"Mmhm," Naomi said with a knowing look. Rose blushed. She was having to do a lot of that in the company we'd been keeping, with the things we'd had to explain to some of them, lately.

"So that I can cast the parts of the consorting spell," she clarified.

"Of course, of course. Is there anything else in here you'll need?"

"I don't think so."

"Well, if you do think of anything, just let me know." Naomi hesitated, and her expression turned suddenly serious. "The thought of what your dad did to you, or at least tried to do—snuff my spark, I can't even imagine it. I wish we'd been there for you earlier. But you're not getting rid of me now, cuz."

She knocked Rose's arm with her own in playful affection.

"Thank you," Rose said, sounding happy and uncertain at the same time.

Naomi ambled off, and Rose came to stand beside me in the doorway. "What's up?" she asked, worry shadowing her face. The sight of it made my chest ache. She'd been carrying those shadows for a long time now, but in the last few hours I'd gotten the sense they were weighing on her even more than usual.

"Nothing's wrong," I reassured her. "I just wanted to see you. To find out if there's anything I can do for you. You've been wearing yourself out, all this running around."

She shrugged. "I needed to prepare for the ceremony. If it's going to work, I have to make sure I do everything right."

"It'll work." I touched her cheek, tracing my thumb across her cheekbone. "I can feel it."

She raised an eyebrow at me, but the corner of her lips quirked up. "And you're now the expert on magical possibilities?"

"I think anything is possible when you're the one casting the spell."

She let out a little groan and tipped her head toward me. I wrapped my arms around her as she rested her forehead on my shoulder.

"I wish it were that simple, Jin," she said. "Now I'm

getting all these other people mixed up in our problems too. And they're being so *nice* to me about it."

"You're family," I said. "That's what good families do. It's just too bad you didn't know you had one like this over here all this time."

"Yeah."

"You seem to be getting along pretty well with Naomi."

"She's nice too. And she seems to be more excited than judgy about the possibilities of multiple consorts." Rose laughed against my shirt. "Also, she reads. You should see the bookcase in her room. Not half as big as mine, but—well, there's a lot of overlap between our collections, let's just say."

"All those romances that have corrupted your innocent mind," I teased.

She gave me a little shove, grinning at me. But before I could give in to the urge to kiss her like I wanted to, her expression fell again. She needed more from me than just physical affection. I reached for the right thing to say.

"You picked the spot we're going to do the ceremony, didn't you? Will you show me?"

"All right."

Her hand curled around mine as she led me through the house. After all her bustling around getting ready, she walked through the halls as confidently as if she'd been visiting here for years.

The gardens out back were as big as the ones on the Hallowell estate, but wilder: rose bushes clambering over random lattices and wildflowers left to bloom around the bases of the pear and plum trees. Together they gave off a pungent floral scent. Rose skirted them on her way into the sparsely wooded area at the back of the property. The longer grass there whispered under her feet.

She stopped in a little clearing about five minutes from the house and turned around. I turned with her, taking the space in. The trees were spaced far enough apart to let warm sunlight stream down, so grass carpeted the ground beneath us. But we'd come far enough that they hid the house and any sign of what else might lie beyond them in every direction. Privacy without feeling too closed in.

"It's perfect," I said.

"I thought so too." She dragged in a breath and let it out slow. Gently, she set down the bowl with her supplies at the base of one of the trees. "I do want you all to be there. I meant that. I think you should be a part of the ceremony just like you were the first time, even if this one is mostly about Gabriel."

"Absolutely. You know we want to be a part of this... collective? In every way."

She chuckled at my choice of words. "Quite a collective it's becoming. But maybe once I have that bond with Gabriel, and with Aunt Ginny's family on our side... Maybe there is a chance we can push back that faction of the Assembly and put down roots somewhere."

"I think there's more than a chance," I said. "But you need to give yourself space to breathe too, Rose. It's not all on you."

When her mouth slanted down as if she meant to argue, I motioned her closer. "Come here." Hooking my hand around her elbow, I sat us down on the grass and then lay back. Rose made a vague sound of protest but followed me anyway. I kept my arm looped around hers and gestured with my other hand toward the sky.

"Look at the way the sunlight shimmers as it passes through the leaves. Look at how fucking blue that sky is. This is yours, right now. Personally, I don't think there's any point in even being alive if we don't stop and absorb the beauty around us when we have a moment to."

Rose was silent for a minute. "It is beautiful," she said. "You're right." Some of the tension had ebbed from her voice. She twined her fingers with mine. "And I have a family I didn't even know anything about a few days ago—a family that wants to support me."

"A cousin who likes the same books you do."

"I'll be able to sleep in not just a bed but a comfortable one tonight."

"And you have five hot and charming, if I do say so myself, guys who'll happily share that bed with you."

She laughed and rolled onto her side to sling her arm around my waist. "It's pretty amazing, isn't it, how much good there can be even when everything seems totally wrong?"

"You're pretty amazing," I told her. But the joy I'd been looking for had come back into her eyes. Her shoulders were no longer tight. The ache I'd felt before dissolved into a wash of warmth.

I'd worried in the past that I wasn't taking things seriously enough, that I was focusing too much on how to make Rose happy and not enough on what would keep her safe. But there was room for both, wasn't there? And this was the part I was good at. This was the part I loved.

Bringing a smile to her face, knowing I'd lit a little awe and pleasure inside her.

Of course, there were ways I could add to that pleasure.

This time I didn't hold myself back. I rolled to meet her, capturing her lips with mine. Rose sighed happily into the kiss, her fingers teasing up the back of my neck with a heady tingle through my skin. Her mouth tasted like the fresh pears we'd been eating at lunch time.

I kissed her again and then trailed my lips down her jaw to her neck, reveling in the hitch of her breath, the scoot of her body to press even closer to mine.

"What do you say we take this spot out for a little trial run?" I said.

Her giggle, light as anything, was a victory in itself. "I'd say that sounds like a very good idea," she said, and pulled my mouth back to hers.

CHAPTER NINETEEN

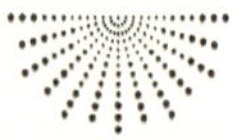

Rose

It felt strange walking out between the trees of Aunt Ginny's estate under the pale light of the waning moon. So different from the first consort ceremony I'd orchestrated. All the fears that had been hanging over me then, all the need for secrecy—that was gone.

I still had fears, but they were new ones. And this time I walked together with my consorts and the man I'd soon also be consorted to. This time there was no uncertainty about what they'd say, how they'd respond to the idea. The only unknown was whether the great Spark, the light of all our lives, would let me accept another partner.

Gabriel walked next to me, his hand around mine. When we reached the clearing, I paused. The pleasantly cool night breeze rustled through the leaves overhead and licked over the simple dress I'd chosen, carrying the smell of wildflowers from the garden.

The other guys came to a stop around us, watching me in the near darkness. Anticipation hung in the air so thickly I could almost taste it, tart and electric on my tongue.

All that preparation, and I still wasn't completely sure where to start.

Gabriel gave my hand a gentle tug, turning me toward him. He bent his head so his forehead grazed mine. His voice came out low but steady.

"I want this. I want you. I don't have a single doubt about that. In case you needed to hear it again."

I swallowed hard and touched his jaw to bring him in for a kiss. His words and the hot press of his mouth against mine brought a rush of love into my chest.

The Spark had to see how much he meant to me—to all of us. How could there be anything wrong with making the bond that was already there so much more concrete?

As I stepped back, Damon coughed. "If you need any help feeding that magic of yours ahead of time..."

I glanced at him, and he grinned wickedly. Oh, he'd helped feed my spark before our last ceremony quite well. It burned brightly behind my ribs already, stoked by all the intimacies I'd shared with my four consorts in the last couple days since I'd started holding my magicking in check. But a little more couldn't hurt. They should all be part of this ceremony.

"Maybe I need a taste from all of you," I said with a smile.

I held out my hand, and Damon swooped in, but the others were right behind. As my reckless rebel claimed my mouth, Seth bent to press his lips to the side of my neck. Kyler nipped my earlobe. Jin traced his fingers down my side and leaned in to steal a kiss for himself when Damon eased back.

My spark danced with a brilliant flare of light and heat that blazed all through my body. I hadn't needed that extra boost, but my feet felt firmer beneath me now.

I motioned my consorts to the edge of the small clearing. "I suppose the best thing is for you to make a ring around us. Witness the ceremony. I'll let you know if I think there's any other way you should step in."

Seth nodded, and they all stepped back. It was just Gabriel and me left in the middle.

"I just do what we talked about earlier?" he said.

"That's all there is to it. Mostly you just follow my cues." I trailed my fingers down his face, holding those bright blue eyes, for one more moment. Bending down, I found the sticks of charcoal and lengths of cord I'd left there. I handed Gabriel's to him and tucked my own into my pocket. Then I stepped back like the others had, to give myself room to perform the first of the spells.

My body moved into the motions even more easily than the first time, knowing the right feel of it, knowing how the magic would come together. I shifted my feet over the grass and unfurled my arms toward the sky, then back down along my body, channeling all the magic I had in me to the edges of my body. Offering it up to the great Spark that warmed us all.

The words spilled from my lips as if the magic

propelled them. "The Spark that guides us, bless this partnering."

I swept the bowl Naomi had lent me up from the grass and swiveled as I raised it over my head. My dress swished around me with the slow circle of my turn. My magic tingled up through my arms. I held the bowl toward the sky as if the whole world would fill it. Then I brought it to my mouth as if to taste the magic I'd sent into it.

That sense of power tingled over my tongue. I offered the bowl to Gabriel. He opened his mouth as I tipped it, drinking in the same symbolic communion. A quiver of energy passed from him into me, and my breath caught.

That was the first time his essence had touched my spark. My first glimpse of what our bond might feel like. It wasn't as urgent or heady as the sensation had been during my first consorting, but before then my spark hadn't been properly kindled at all. Just to feel my connection with Gabriel solidifying made my spirits soar.

I set the bowl down and whirled again, sending a wave of magic through the clearing, wrapping it around the two of us and touching my other consorts as well. My spin stopped with me facing Gabriel. I took out my stick of charcoal and held it toward him.

Gabriel had his ready in his hand. He raised it to touch its tip to mine. I stared at the point of contact and willed a flicker of magic through my fingers.

The charcoal was meant to light with a literal flame. But nothing happened. I frowned and urged another jolt of heat toward the sticks with a wave of my other hand.

The night air seemed to swallow that energy up. My pulse thumped harder. Why wasn't this working?

Gabriel watched me, looking calm and confident as always. He was so sure that I'd find a way to finish this ceremony, to make our connection as deep as it should be. What was wrong wasn't with him.

No, it was in me. A prickling crept through my nerves with little jabs of heat as my spark sputtered toward each of the four guys in their ring around us, pulled in four directions at the same time.

I drew in a breath, settling my thoughts. Maybe I needed them to be more a part of this ceremony than I'd realized.

"Consorts of mine," I said, improvising as I went. "Will you bless this union too?"

I reached my stick of charcoal toward Seth, the closest at my left. He dipped his head, every inch of his powerful body showing nothing but approval. "You and Gabriel have my blessing. Let's all join together."

He was improvising too, but the words echoed the ones we'd used in our consort ceremony. A little of the jittering inside me eased. I pointed to Kyler next.

"You and Gabriel have my blessing," he said, smiling. "Let's all join together."

Damon was next. Amusement glinted in his dark eyes. "You and Gabriel have my blessing. Let's all join together."

When I turned to Jin, he was beaming. "You and Gabriel have my blessing. Let's all join together."

The last of that uncomfortable prickling fell away. My spark glowed with an eager pulse and seemed to reach toward Gabriel now. I met my new consort-to-be's gaze, a smile stretching across my own face. When I touched my charcoal stick to his now, with a twitch of my fingers a flame leapt up between them. A flare of longing shot from my core at the same time. Gabriel's eyes widened with a glimmer of awe.

"With you I would kindle my spark," I said. "Will you join me?"

"I will," Gabriel said, with so much weight and longing in those two words that my heart swelled.

His acceptance sent a thrum of power through the clearing around us. It sang in my ears as I lifted my charcoal stick into the air, stirring up even more desire. Gabriel copied my gesture.

"We will honor the Spark with our bond," I said.

"We will honor the Spark with our bond," he recited in turn. The flames on our sticks leapt higher, blazing against the dark. Energy raced down my arm and tickled around my torso, hot and needy.

Now I had to seal that bond I'd opened between us. I lowered the charcoal and snuffed out the flame against my palm. The fire on Gabriel's vanished in the same instant.

As I had with the four guys around us weeks ago now, I drew the glyph for joining on my palm and guided Gabriel through its lines on his own. The feel of his skin against mine made me quiver with eagerness. Then I set one end of the white cord Naomi had given me on his marked hand.

"I, Rosalind Hallowell, take Gabriel Lorde as my consort," I said. He gripped the cord as I did, and magic raced giddily between us. My voice reverberated with it when I added, "I will light my spark by him and never let it burn him."

Gabriel held out his own length of cord, the blue one, for me to grasp in turn. "I, Gabriel Lorde, take Rosalind Hallowell as my consort." He paused, his gaze burning into mine as magic surged through us both. "I will light her spark with my heart and never do her harm."

A sharper rush of joy whipped through me. I had to swallow hard to contain the emotion. I hadn't told him to say that. It wasn't part of the official ceremony. But the other guys had added it in during theirs. One of them must have told him, so he could become a part of our group in exactly the same way.

The bond between us snapped into place alongside my joy. Every nerve in my body rang with the magic of it. Heat pooled in my chest and low in my belly, and a pleased laugh fell from Gabriel's lips as he must have felt the same sensation. Then I was wrapping my arm around his neck and pulling him into a kiss.

There wasn't any need to wait this time. No need to hold back from the whirlwind of passion that our joining had stirred between us. I gave myself over to my desire without hesitation.

"Rose," Gabriel murmured against my mouth, and then he was kissing me even harder. We stumbled to the edge of the clearing, my back hitting a tree. He pressed me against it, his lips scorching along my jaw and neck, his hands tugging up my dress.

I wrenched his shirt off of him with the pop of a snapped button. Oh well. I could buy him a new one.

Right now I wanted—I *needed*—to feel all that hot hard muscled body beneath my hands.

He groaned as I explored his chest. His fingers dipped inside my panties to stroke the most sensitive part of me. I gasped as he flicked his thumb over my inflamed clit.

My spark was searing through every part of my body now. All I could think of was joining with this man completely, in the most physical possible way.

He yanked my panties down, and I fumbled with the fly of his jeans. Then he was pushing me up against the tree again, hefting my thighs around his hips, his mouth crashing back into mine. The rough bark rasped against the bare skin at the top of my back, but that hint of pain only brought the pleasure of his touch into brighter relief.

His cock filled me with one hot thrust and a wave of deeper pleasure. I moaned, bucking my hips to meet him. With every stutter of his breath, every caress of his hands, every plunge deeper inside me, magic twined between us even more strongly.

"My Gabriel," I murmured. "My consort."

He let out a choked sound. "From now until always, Rose."

He picked up his pace even more, our bodies coming together at an almost frantic rhythm. His hand closed over my breast with a flick of my nipple through the dress's fabric, and somehow that was what sent me over the edge.

Pleasure spiked through my nerves. I cried out, and Gabriel closed his mouth over mine, drinking in my release with a few more jerks of his hips. Then he came too, with a rough gasp. He rocked against me, his rhythm slowing, until we came to a stop braced against the tree, breathing hard, lost in the hazy afterglow of bliss.

Footsteps whispered over the grass. My other consorts came up around us, touching my shoulder, my face—forming a tighter circle around us. An embrace, all six of us together, as if we were just one body, one being. I leaned my head to the side against Seth's shoulder, squeezed Jin's fingers, and slipped my other hand around Gabriel's neck to keep him close against me.

It was done. Whatever else the Assembly threw at us, whatever else lay ahead, no one could shake the ties I'd formed with the guys who'd always felt like my destiny.

CHAPTER TWENTY

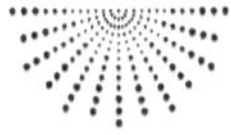

Rose

"Oh, you *absolutely* have to try Tilda Carrington's regencies," Naomi said between bites of breakfast croissant. "If you like Cadence Marsten, you'll love Tilda's stuff."

I laughed around my own mouthful of buttery pastry. "Well, how can I say no to a recommendation like that?"

"And there is one author I've read who writes about women with multiple partners... Who was that again? Oh, I'll have to look through my collection to find it. But maybe that would appeal?" My cousin raised her eyebrows.

Warmth crept into my cheeks, but at the same time I couldn't help thinking that scenes in those books might give me a little inspiration in certain areas. Inadvertently, my gaze drifted to the guys sitting around the table with us.

Kyler had clearly been listening in. He met my gaze with a grin. "You know I'm always a fan of research."

Damon's head jerked up over the heap of bacon he'd been inhaling. "What are we researching now?" he demanded.

Ky opened his mouth to answer, and the doorbell rang, followed almost immediately by a sharp rapping. I stiffened in my seat, and all five of my consorts tensed. Naomi's brow creased for the few seconds before a muffled but strident voice carried through the door and down the hall with the knocking.

"Ginny? We need to speak immediately."

"That's Aunt Irene," Naomi said to me under her breath. "She's not very good at taking no for an answer. Or things like calling ahead rather than showing up unannounced."

My shoulders came down, but my pulse was still skittering. "Should we be worried about her? She wouldn't turn us over to the Assembly, would she?"

"I don't think so," Naomi said. "She's a bit of a hardass, but she's not, like, malicious. She'd never do anything to hurt the family. And I know she was wrapped up in the case with Grandma and Gramps when they were trying to reach out to your mom and then investigate her death. I've heard her and Mom talking about it a few times. She definitely didn't like your dad at all."

Aunt Ginny had obviously heard her sister's call. Footsteps pattered down the hall. The door sighed open. Whatever she said to Aunt Irene, it was too quiet for us to make out all the way over in the breakfast room.

"They called me right up," Irene replied, her voice even harder to ignore now that there wasn't a door between her and us toning it down. "Wanted to know about Rose—said she might have come to see us, that she might have several *unsparked men* with her?" She sounded incredulous and either impressed or horrified. It was hard to tell which. I had a bad feeling I knew who "they" were, though. Our enemies hadn't been totally convinced we'd left the city if they were still poking around here.

The conversation continued at more of a hush. I set down the rest of my croissant, no longer hungry. The pastry's sweetness had soured in my mouth.

Gabriel reached over and set his hand over mine. Meeting my newest consort's gaze, absorbing the reassurance of his touch, my nerves settled a little.

Whatever happened, we were in this together. Completely, now.

A moment later, an imperious woman swept into the room with Aunt Ginny at her heels. My mother's older sister—because who else could this woman be—radiated an air of authority from where her gray-streaked black hair was pulled into a twist on the top of her head to the buckles of her loafers. She fixed her eyes, the same dark green as mine and my mother's, on me in an instant.

"So, she is here," she said, and took in the rest of the figures around the table too. "And the men too."

My heart thumped faster, but I pushed myself to my feet and pasted a smile onto my face. "Aunt Irene? It's so good to finally meet you. And to be able to introduce you to my consorts."

Irene's eyebrows arched. She gave me a crooked smile in return. "Alora's Rose. What strange things you've gotten yourself into out there on the west coast. It appears we have a lot to talk about."

* * *

When I'd finished telling Aunt Irene my story, she just looked at me for longer than felt completely comfortable. We'd moved into the living room, ending up in almost the same positions as when I'd given this account to Aunt Ginny's family yesterday, except only Aunt Ginny and Naomi had joined the Levesque side of the room this time. Naomi had given me supported nods while I'd been talking. It had been a little easier the second time, as intimidating as my older aunt was.

"We've seen signs of it ourselves, haven't we?" Aunt Ginny spoke up. "I've been thinking about it ever since Rose told me all this—there was Helen Osler, the way she got quieter during that first year of her marriage, and she faded out of the get-togethers with the rest of us... We thought she was just wrapped up in her new life, but maybe it wasn't a good sort of wrapped up. I haven't even heard from her in years now."

"And Rhiannon Wells," Irene said, her face drawn. "I have to wonder about her too. There was something about the consort she ended up with... I talked to her once after the move, and something in her voice..." She shook her head. "But that isn't the most important matter of the moment. The most important matter is that you're harboring six people the Assembly has named as criminals, even if most of the members don't have the full story. They already suspect Rose might be here."

"You said you got a call," I ventured.

She didn't seem bothered by my admitting I'd listened in on that conversation. Maybe she realized it was hard to expect anyone not to, at the volume she liked to talk.

"A representative from the Justice division wanted to make me aware of the 'situation' and find out if you'd been in contact," she said. "I told her you hadn't, naturally, because you hadn't. But I'm sure this is the next place they'll be checking. I'm surprised they haven't already given you a call." She glanced at her sister.

"They must have assumed you'd know all there is to know about the goings-on in the Levesque family," Aunt Ginny said with a slightly teasing note in her voice. "Owen, Greg, and the girls know not to mention anything outside this house. We've been careful."

"But if we know witches who might have had their magic bound like Rose's father tried to do with hers," Naomi said. "If it could be happening to *other* witches, witches my age who are just preparing to get consorted now—we have to stand up to them, don't we? What if one of these predators sucked in Stella?"

Ginny's jaw tightened. Of course she was worried about her younger daughter.

Irene let out a huff. From what I'd gathered, her only daughter was twenty-nine and already long consorted, and I supposed she didn't need to worry about her son, who was twenty-one, getting tied up in some sort of trap.

"You haven't had many opportunities to go against

the Assembly," she said to my cousin. "I watched everything your grandparents went through for Alora—and it all came to nothing. If you go after the Assembly and you don't have an absolutely solid case, you're as likely to be crushed as anything. Your grandfather lost half of his business clients over that matter. We nearly lost the *estate*, with that sudden drop in income."

"I'm not asking you to fight for me," I said. "We just needed somewhere to take shelter while we prepared for whatever we're going to do next. And to find out if you had any proof or information we could use."

"We don't have a whole lot of choice about what *we* do," Seth put in. "Either we fight, or we let them take us. And the second option probably ends with us all dead."

Damon had his arms crossed over his chest, his expression wary. "Yeah. They brought the fight to us. We didn't ask for it."

"You simply being here implicates us, you know," Aunt Irene said to me, ignoring the guys.

"She's our niece," Aunt Ginny protested. "We owe her at least this much."

"We don't even know the girl." Irene looked at me. "I'm just stating the facts. You dropped into our lives out of nowhere."

My stomach balled into a knot, but I managed to nod. "I understand. I wish I hadn't needed to impose like this."

"It's fine," Ginny said. She raised her chin. "You don't have to get involved, Irene. You didn't have to come over at all. I kept you out of it because I didn't think you'd like the risks, and obviously I had the right idea."

"The whole family assumes the risk even if you don't

tell me," Irene said. She sighed, looking weary for a fleeting moment before she raised her chin again. "Here we are now. Let's see what we can make of this muddle. Rose, perhaps you can—"

A new ring of the doorbell cut her off. We all glanced at each other. "Are you expecting anyone?" Irene asked Ginny.

My younger aunt shook her head. "And you're already here, so that eliminates the usual random visitor."

Irene glowered at her. Naomi got to her feet. "Well, we'd better answer it."

Ginny sucked in a breath. She motioned to her daughter. "We can't take any chances. Take Rose and her consorts upstairs—show them the trap door to the attic. If you have to hide anywhere, that's the best place. There's a dormer that'll let you out onto the roof if it comes to that. And Naomi, you can run interference to give them time if anyone comes upstairs."

"You're assuming it's the Assembly," Naomi said.

"I just know it could be. Go on."

She hustled toward the front hall as the six of us hurried after my cousin up the stairs. Naomi opened the door to what I took to be Aunt Ginny and Uncle Owen's master bedroom. At the back of the walk-in closet, a small square was etched in the ceiling.

"You have to pull over the chest and climb up on it to get up there," Naomi said. She grasped the edge of the chest and tugged. "Here, I'll get it in place now. Stella and I used to goof around up there as kids. Not much to see except a few pieces of old furniture and some boxes of stuff we never use." She looked at me, her eyes worried. "You'll be okay?"

"We don't even know if it's someone looking for us at the door," I said, but my gut was still tight.

"I guess we'd better find out. We might be able to hear them from the landing. But as soon as it sounds like they might come up, you'd better head for the attic. Come on."

CHAPTER TWENTY-ONE

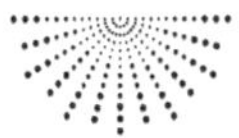

Seth

We sat in a cluster near the top of the stairs, ears perked as voices carried from the first floor.

"Well, it's certainly a surprise to be having a couple members of the Assembly dropping by out of the blue," Rose's Aunt Ginny was saying with a quick laugh I was relieved to hear didn't sound forced.

She was purposefully calling attention to her visitors' status for our benefit, I realized. Knowing we were probably listening in to determine the danger. A flicker of gratitude slipped through me. I hadn't been all that impressed by Rose's witching society so far, but this part of her family seemed like good people.

"I apologize for the intrusion," a male voice said in return. Rose stiffened beside me. I recognized it too. It was the man who'd confronted us in Manhattan, the one with the beakish nose and the red-brown hair, for the "parlay" that had quickly devolved into a gun fight thanks to Damon.

Well, and thanks to the Assembly guy too. Maybe I wasn't keen on Damon's over-the-top methods, but I could see why he'd felt he needed to act.

We all did whatever we could to protect Rose in our own ways.

All six of us and Rose's cousin Naomi kept our lips tightly shut as the voices traveled from the hall into one of the side rooms below. "I'm afraid it's a bit of a delicate matter," the Assembly guy was saying. "I'll try not to take too much of your time."

"We'd just finished up breakfast anyway," Ginny said. "Did you need to speak to Owen too? He's about to head into the office."

"No, no, that's all right. I see your sister has come over. Perhaps she's already informed you of some of our concerns. I also wanted to ask you about a major magicking we noticed emanating from your property last night."

Naomi's mouth tightened. "Don't worry," she murmured to Rose. "Mom already thought of a thorough explanation for the spell we cast to stop them from noticing *your* magicking." But a thread of worry wove through her words.

"Should we go up into the attic?" Rose asked.

Naomi shook her head. "Let's wait and see how this goes. If they really do just want to talk, no point in making a commotion up here."

My brother leaned over, his voice pitched low. "Can't

they force your mother and Irene to tell the truth? Isn't there a spell for that?"

"They'd need reasonable proof of wrongdoing and an order from the high Assembly court, or they'd be using illegal magic too," Rose said. "If they were sure Ginny was harboring us, I'm thinking this faction wouldn't care about that, but it doesn't sound as if they're sure at all."

"So they're playing it cautious," Naomi added. She glanced over at Kyler. "We may not be in the trendy west coast witching crowd, but our family has a long history and plenty of magic to call on. They wouldn't want to be careless with us." Even though she still sounded nervous, a fierce sparkle had lit in her eyes.

The conversation below had faded out, muffled by the walls as they'd moved deeper into the house. I resisted the restless urge to shift my weight. Ginny had indicated there were only two Assembly people here, and at least the guy couldn't use magic on his own. Though I guessed he might have one of those batons. But even so, if it came down to some kind of fight, we had four powerful witches on our side.

It wasn't so much whether we could survive the next hour as how we'd survive if we had to reveal our hand that far. And I knew Rose didn't want to get her mother's family in that kind of trouble. She was biting her lip, her fingers worrying at the hem of the blue cotton blouse Naomi had lent her.

Several minutes passed in that tense silence. Then Ginny called up, "Naomi, Stella, would you mind coming down for a moment? We've got a visitor who needs to speak with you."

Naomi scrambled up. "Just a second, Mom," she called back. Then she turned to Rose and patted her pocket with her phone. "I'll send you an SOS text if you need to get going. But if you feel safer, you can go up to the attic now. Just make sure you're quiet about it."

Her younger sister emerged from her room down the hall. Naomi ducked her head close as they went to the staircase, presumably filling Stella in on everything she'd missed. Stella's eyes widened. She nodded and shot a quick smile our way.

Rose looked around at us, a question in her gaze. Stay here or really go into hiding. I hesitated, not liking either option. The thought of being shut up in the attic with only a dormer window for escape made my skin creep.

"Let's pull back into the bedroom," Gabriel murmured. "Leave the door open so we can still hear if anything major happens."

As one being, we got up and eased across the hall to the master bedroom. Rose slipped into the closet and hopped onto the chest so she could push open the trap door. "In case we need to head up there in a hurry," she said. "Maybe the rest of you should go up ahead—"

Damon was already shaking his head. "We're sticking with you, angel."

She frowned, but she didn't press the issue. Her fingers curled into her palms. I wondered how much it bothered her having all that magic in her but feeling it wasn't safe to use it. She could have sent those Assembly people off in an instant if she'd wanted to. It just wasn't worth the consequences.

Her phone vibrated in the pocket of her jeans with a

faint hum. Rose flinched and reached for it, waving us toward the closet. Then she let out her breath.

"They're leaving the house," she said. "The Assembly people and my family. Naomi didn't have time to say why, but she promised she'll text us when they're heading back so we know when to be on guard again."

As she spoke, the thud of the front door carried from downstairs. I exhaled some of my tension in a rush and reached to pull Rose to me.

She melted into my embrace. I hadn't realized how tense *she'd* been until that moment. I tucked my head close to hers and stroked my hand up and down her back, encouraging her to let go of it all.

It wasn't right that someone so powerful should feel this scared.

"I'm going to go grab a few things to be ready if they do come back," Damon said, his expression dark.

Jin raised an eyebrow. "Things that shoot bullets?"

Damon glowered at him. "You can have one too if you know how to use it."

The other guy raised his hands. "I'll stick to working with paintbrushes and clay, thanks."

"I've got the general idea," Ky said. "Can I at least take a look?"

I stared at my twin. "Where did you learn how to shoot?"

He laughed. "Where do you think? The internet can teach you anything. I'm just not sure how comfortable I'd feel using that information with a real live gun."

"Well, c'mon," Damon said. "Have a look, see what you think."

"You know, I'm actually curious to see what exactly you've picked up," Jin said. "I'll tag along."

Damon rolled his eyes but didn't protest. The three of them headed out of the room. Rose snuggled deeper into my arms.

"I wish I could think the Assembly will finish their little talk and then leave Aunt Ginny alone, and we could just stay here somehow," she said.

"I know. But we'll find a place one way or another," I said. "I'm not letting that house back home stay empty after all the work I put into it."

She looked up at me, her mouth twisting. "It is a beautiful house. It's perfect. Even if that one day is the only day we'll have gotten to use it."

The sadness in her voice wrenched at me. I bent my head to kiss her. She slid her hands behind my neck, kissing me back, and I didn't care that Gabriel was still in the room, leaning against the doorframe while he studied the layout of the hall, or that some new text might come in at any moment telling us we had to run again. Everything was Rose, and that was enough for me.

My cock hardened as her body pressed closer against mine. She kissed me harder, my hands started to ease up under her shirt—and a splinter of pain shot up my spine.

I eased back, resting my head against hers. My breath was coming a little ragged, and not just from the heat of that moment. I'd felt pressure and prickles of discomfort before, in the many times we'd come together in the last week, but I'd been able to ignore them. That splinter had been a little too sharp.

"Maybe not the best time to get too distracted," Rose

said in a playful tone. She didn't know why I'd pulled back. Good.

"Probably not," I agreed.

She gave me one more quick kiss, a brush of her lips against mine. "I suppose I'd better see what Damon's up to before all my consorts are armed and dangerous."

I chuckled. "Left to his own devices, you never know what he'll do."

Rose touched Gabriel's arm on her way past him, and he smiled and grasped her hand briefly in return. But he stayed there with me as she hurried down the hall. After a moment, he looked at me.

"You've been going to her a lot," he said. "More than anyone else."

It didn't sound like an accusation, just an observation, but some part of me bristled anyway. I willed down the impulse to make a hasty defense.

"It's the best thing I can do for her," I said. "Physical comfort, helping her magic. And, I mean, we both enjoy it, so..."

Gabriel's lips quirked up, but his gaze stayed serious. "She's used a lot of magic since the Assembly caught us. We can all help stop her from exhausting herself. The last few days I've just noticed that afterward you've looked more exhausted than usual. A little worn down. And when you stopped just now—it wasn't just because you're worried about them coming back right away, was it?"

Shit. I hadn't thought the effects had been strong enough that anyone had noticed. Maybe they'd been stronger than *I'd* noticed. I had been feeling sluggish in the last few days, but I'd put that down to all the stress of being on the run.

"I don't mind," I said. "I'll give her as much as I can."

"I'm just saying, you don't need to push yourself to the point where it's hurting you," Gabriel said mildly. "She had three other consorts and now she has four. Does she know it's been affecting you?"

I gave him a look. "Do you think she'd even be kissing me if I'd let on?"

"Seth..." Gabriel glanced away for a second and then met my eyes again. "I know I came into this later on than the rest of you. I'm not going to try to tell you I know better. It just seems to me that between the six of us, Rose is the expert on magic. She knows so much more than the rest of us do. So if something to do with the magic or the consorting is a problem... isn't it better if she knows so *she* can decide the best way to deal with that?"

A weight sank into my stomach. "She's already dealing with so much."

"I know." Gabriel rubbed a hand over his face. "Believe me, I know that debate way too well. Do you think I wanted to ask her to take the risk of doing that consort ceremony? It brought the Assembly right back here. But the risks of not telling her what was going on were worse. And I trust her to know what she can and can't handle."

Don't you? He didn't need to say the question or even hint at it. I wet my lips. "I do too. I just..."

I wanted to protect her. I wanted to be the strong one, the rock she could rely on. But I wouldn't really be that if one day I suddenly cracked under a strain I hadn't fully understood.

I sighed. "Okay. Point taken. Thanks."

Gabriel shrugged, pushing himself off the doorframe. "I figure we all have to look out for each other. We're all looking out for Rose. And we've got to let her look out for us—and to look out for each other. I felt that, last night, during the ceremony. The caring, the connection, doesn't just go from us to her. It's all of us, joined together. Or maybe it only seemed that way in the moment." He gave me a wry smile.

I had to smile back. "No, I've felt that too." I paused. "You know, I'm glad you did come back. I'm glad you're here. We work better when it's all six of us, don't we?"

Gabriel's smile softened. "Yeah," he said. "I think we do. Should we see what the others are up to?"

I followed him out of the room, my spirits a little lighter but that weight still in my gut. I didn't think it was going to shift until I found a way to talk to Rose. And even if I trusted her, I already knew it wasn't going to be a fun conversation.

If I'd been smart, I'd have told her in the first place. Too late for that now.

CHAPTER TWENTY-TWO

Rose

When Aunt Ginny's family got back a couple hours later, it was just her and my cousins. "The Assembly peeps went off to do their corrupt Assembly things," Naomi summarized for me breezily as she guided me into her room for a private talk. "And Aunt Irene went home, at least for the moment. She threatened that she'd come for dinner."

"I'm getting the impression you don't get along with her so well," I said.

"Oh, well, you know... She just takes being the matriarch of the family *very* seriously." Naomi wrinkled her nose. Then she motioned for me to sit down at her reading desk while she sat on the edge of her bed across from me. The comforting smell of slowly aging paper drifted from the bookshelf behind me. I tried to focus on that and not the anxiety I could sense from my cousin under her flippant tone.

"I know we have to leave," I said. That thought had loomed large in my mind while I'd waited for the family to return. "I've put all of you in enough danger already. It's not as if you could hide us away forever. If you don't have anything we can use to make the Assembly back off, well, we'll just have to find some other way to do it. We've got other strategies we can use to try to gain some leverage."

Naomi blinked at me. "You know, I was going to suggest the exact same thing—that you should leave and look into other strategies. But not like that. I think *we* should go take on this wretched faction that thinks enslaving witches is the thing to do."

"We?" I repeated, staring at her.

"Yes," she said firmly. "You and me and your consorts —and mine. I already talked to Greg. He agrees with me. And if things get bad, I suppose I might need him for more than just emotional support." She let out a rough laugh. "I can mask any magic you need to use along the way. And the two of us should be able to accomplish plenty more than just one, even if you've got the fuel of five consorts."

"But..." I grasped for the right thing to say. "It isn't your fight. You hardly know me."

"I know you well enough," Naomi said with a swish of her chestnut ponytail. "I know you're family. And I know what your father did, with the help of these people —they've hurt a lot more than just you."

"But when they find out you're helping me, and they

almost definitely will, they could ruin your whole future."

"Not if we ruin theirs first," Naomi said, so fiercely that the nervous flutter in my chest started to fade. Maybe she was prepared for this kind of battle after all.

My cousin paused and leaned forward on the bed. Her brown eyes held mine. "And it's not just the principle of the thing, Rose. The truth is... There was a while when I wasn't sure I'd find a guy I really wanted as a consort. When I thought I'd have to choose between taking some guy I was iffy about or losing my magic."

"Really?" I said. Snuff my spark, I knew how awful that uncertainty was. It'd been creeping up on me most of the last few years.

She shrugged. "Our family is respected, sure, and everyone knows we come into a lot of power, but we're also seen as a little odd. My mom told me a few times, 'Everyone wants to marry into the Levesques, but not all that many want to marry a Levesque.'" She gave me a slanted smile.

"But you found Greg."

"I did," she said. "And I feel very lucky about that. But, you know... We got married faster than I'd have really liked, just because I wanted to make sure I didn't lose him. Everything's good now, but we've only been together a couple of years. We've only been married for five months. Sometimes I wonder what would happen if we grew apart after all... Don't tell him I said that. I'd bet he's thought about the same things too."

"I don't think there's anything wrong with wondering that," I said.

"No. Well." She looked at her hands. "Hearing what happened to you, I know how easily that could have been me. Duped into consorting with some guy who didn't actually have my best interests at heart. Or what if it happened to Stella? We've got so little time to find that first consort. No one should have to worry that the guys they're getting to know might be trying to trap them. And if more people knew we didn't *have* to pick from witching society, maybe no one would get quite that desperate anyway."

I scooted forward on my chair so I could squeeze her hand. Those memories of all the fears and worries that had weighed on me when I'd known my time was ticking down, when I hadn't yet found a connection with any witching guy I knew, resonated inside me. Naomi acted as if she were impervious a lot of the time, but this fight obviously meant a lot to her, enough for her to make herself vulnerable, too.

"Yeah," I said. "I totally agree. And I'll change that if I can. I suppose, if you want to come with me, I can't really say no. It'd be good to have a little relief from the testosterone now and then."

Her smile came back at those last words. "I can only imagine," she said, winking at me. Then she leapt up. "All right. How soon do you think we should leave?"

"I thought we'd sneak out tonight," I said. "When it's dark, it'll be easier to conceal ourselves if the Assembly people are watching the estate."

She nodded. "That makes sense. I can manage that. Let me talk to Mom first so she doesn't feel blindsided, and then I'll get packing."

She bounded out of the room, her ponytail swinging behind her. As the door clicked shut, a presence formed at my left, standing by the bed.

I turned my head toward Philomena. She looked even more filmy than she had the last time she'd appeared. But the pink of the ruffled dress she was wearing this time was still bright, as was her grin.

"I just wanted to say good-bye," she said. "We've had a long good time of it, haven't we, Rose?"

I jerked all the way around, my pulse hiccupping. "Good-bye?" But even as I said it, I understood. She was only part of my imagination, after all. As much as she'd come to life on her own, in the end everything she knew, I did too.

Phil tipped her head coyly. "You've got your guys now. You've got a new sidekick who can actually help you with more than just chatter. Who's *real*. I know when I've served my purpose. But it didn't seem fair to just disappear without one last chat."

I swallowed hard. It would be silly to cry over an imaginary friend, wouldn't it? I knew I was too old for this. But still...

"I'm going to miss you," I said. "We did have a lot of good times. You were there for me when I needed you."

"That's what's most important." Phil fluttered her fan at me. "Now go enjoy those strapping young men of yours—and don't forget to have some fun even when you're running for your life, you hear."

I blinked, and she was gone. An ache formed in my chest, but at the same time my heart felt even more full.

I got up from the chair to go tell my consorts that we didn't have to set off alone.

* * *

I came downstairs some time later to an argument that had already started. Apparently Aunt Irene had returned early.

"This is ridiculous," she was saying. "You can't just run off with a bunch of fugitives."

"I can, Aunt Irene," Naomi said. "I'm not sure why you think you can decide that for me. I'm a witch with a kindled spark. My life is mine."

"But you have to think about the rest of the family. The sanctions they could bring down on us. Don't you care about your mother? Your future children?"

"Yes," Naomi retorted. "Especially them. I don't want them to end up having to fight for their freedom like Rose is."

"Irene," Ginny said pleadingly, just as I walked in. My older aunt spun toward me instead.

"You've dragged her into this," Aunt Irene said. "Naomi was just settling in to consorting life, and now she's going to charge across the country to take on some supposed conspiracy? What were you thinking?"

My hackles immediately went up. "I didn't drag her. I didn't even *ask* her. She came to me saying she wanted to help—I even tried to talk her out of it."

Irene gave me a skeptical look. "Not very hard, it seems."

"Well, she's twenty-three. She's consorted. She can make up her own mind, can't she?"

"Yes," Naomi put in. "I can. Thank you."

"You..." Irene shook her head. "I think you'd better give us time to talk this through just within the family, Miss Hallowell."

Even though that was the name I'd had my entire life, the way she said, the way she'd used it, stung.

"She *is* family," Naomi protested, but I held up my hand.

"That's fine," I said, my gaze fixed on Irene. "But for next time, it's *Lady* Hallowell."

I turned on my heel. As I left the room, Naomi made a frustrated sound. "I don't want to talk about this anymore. I've already made my decision, and it's mine to make."

She stormed off down the hall, I assumed toward the home office where Greg had been working. I headed upstairs, unsure whether we should even bother sticking around for dinner. But we still had more logistics to work out.

Seth was waiting at the top of the stairs. He must have overheard at least some of that conversation, because when I reached him, he said, "Naomi seems pretty set on coming with us."

"Yeah," I said. "I hope that's a good thing. She could be a lot of help. But I wouldn't have pushed her into it."

"Like you said, she knows her own mind." He paused, and his jaw worked. "There's actually something I thought we should talk about before we leave—while we still have some privacy. Nothing bad, just..."

It was pretty normal for Seth to look serious, but now he looked even more solemn than usual. "What's wrong?" I said.

He motioned me into one of the guest bedrooms. Then he looked at the floor for a moment as if he were trying to gather his words. His gray-green eyes were shadowed. My heart started to sink.

"It's just..." He swallowed hard. "I want you to know that however this comes out, none of it is your fault. It was just me thinking I could handle more than maybe was really wise."

My heart plummeted farther. "What are you talking about?"

Seth set a gentle hand on my shoulder as he raised his head to look at me. "I told you, it's nothing bad. Not that bad, anyway. It's just... I've tried to be there for you a lot in the last week. In lots of, ah, very pleasurable ways." He managed a smile that looked genuine. "But I'm realizing that it's taking a little more out of me than maybe is good for me. With the energy I give to your magic."

My magic, my spark, was lit by the passion we created between us. It wasn't really meant to take away from my consorts. But I'd read stories of witches who expended so much magic their consorts started to suffer during the replenishing. Building that power with me, releasing it to me, could take its toll.

That suffering was just the last thing I'd ever wanted to inflict on any of my consorts.

"What's been happening?" I asked quietly. "How have you been feeling?"

Seth grimaced. "At first it was just a bit of pressure,

just a tiny bit uncomfortable. But that's grown and become more painful. I'm not sure it'd be a good idea for us to do anything... intimate for at least a few days."

He looked so guilty saying that, my heart wrenched. I grasped his arm. "Of course. Seth, I've got four other consorts. If our luck holds, especially with Naomi with us, I won't even need to use so much magic I'd exhaust one consort. The last thing I want is for our bond to be hurting you."

"I know," he said. "That's why I hated to tell you. But obviously you needed to know."

"I did. Thank you. I wouldn't ever want you to keep something like that from me." I dragged in a breath, and a fresh pang ran through my chest. "Don't offer any more than you think is good for you. I won't initiate anything until you give me the go ahead. And any time in the future, if it ever becomes too much again—"

He was already nodding. "I'll speak up. Don't worry. That's why I'm telling you now—so you know that I *will* tell you, and that if I haven't said anything, you can assume I'm fine. I won't pretend I am when I'm not again. You can count on that."

I held his gaze with a little smile of my own. "Promise."

The corner of his lips curved up again. "Should I pinkie swear?"

"I guess it wouldn't hurt."

He hooked his little finger around mine, his face turning serious again. "I swear if anything about your magic is affecting me badly, I'll tell you."

His resolve rang through the words. The wrenching inside me eased, but only partly.

Seth had come to me with this—had been suffering, even if only in a small way, for days. What if he wasn't the only one?

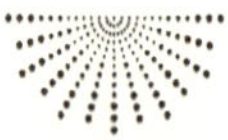

CHAPTER TWENTY-THREE

Rose

"I've got to say again, this is quite the ride," Kyler said, stretching out his arms along the back of the cushioned bench.

The colors of the bus's interior were a little garish, neon blues and greens splattered across the dark gray, but I couldn't complain about it otherwise. It was perfect for our purposes, with the two long comfortable benches at the front behind the driver's area, two sets of curtained bunks beyond them where we could sleep, and another seating area at the very back. We'd swapped in and out of the bunks overnight after we'd started our hasty journey from the Levesque estate.

Naomi laughed. "It's amazing what you can find on short notice around New York City. This was a band tour bus in another life."

Damon sucked in a deep breath. "And I think I can still smell the booze and the weed."

"Give me another few pit stops, and all you'll smell is paint," Jin said with a grin. A faintly tangy scent already hung in the air from the glyphs he'd been painting on the inner walls, using a few sketches I'd done for reference. As he finished each one, Naomi imbued it with protective magic to match the symbol. The goal was to shield and repel any destructive magic that came at us.

"It doesn't maneuver too badly either," Seth said from the driver's seat. He patted the wheel.

Naomi slid her fingers around Greg's hand where he was sitting next to her. Her consort had been taking this whole escapade in with a somewhat bemused expression, but at least he didn't look upset about being here.

"So," she said. "New day, well on our way—let's talk plans. What can we get on this crazy faction of the Assembly to shut them down? And how?"

Gabriel tipped his head to Ky. "You managed to dig up that one incriminating file from their server in Portland. If you could manage to get in there longer..."

Ky nodded. "I've been thinking about that. I'm pretty sure I'd need to go right into the building to get full access. They detected the outside intrusion way too quickly last time. But with a little magic on my side, maybe that won't be a problem." He smiled, but I could tell from the tensing of his shoulders that the idea made him a little nervous.

"Figure out exactly what you'd need as well as you can, and Naomi and I will work out the best way to make that happen," I told him. He shifted his smile directly at me, warmer now.

"And what was that thing the one guy said to you," Damon asked Gabriel. "Something about a cliff?"

"Right!" I said. "We have some idea where that is thanks to Ky's searching before. Charles Frankford has his property out there. If they're doing something they can threaten people with there, it's worth looking into. And they won't expect us to know about it, so that might be a better place to start than trying to waltz right into the Assembly building."

"Cliff?" Naomi said, sounding puzzled.

"When we were being held by the Assembly, one of the enforcers made a comment to me about taking me out to "The Cliff" to terrify me into talking," Gabriel said.

"You've never heard anything about that either?" I asked Naomi.

She shook her head. "Nope. Beats me what that could be. But anything that's going on out west, we're always a little detached from on the east coast. If you didn't know about it, living out there, they must be keeping it really under wraps."

"Like a lot of things," Damon muttered.

Naomi patted her pocket with her phone. "Well, I talked with my mom about the families she knows fairly well. I've got a list of people we're both pretty sure we can trust to at least help once we have some proof."

"Perfect," I said. Now we just had to get that proof.

"Hey," Greg said, tapping the back of the driver's seat. "You've been up there for a while. Why don't we gas up and I'll take over the next stint?"

From the way Seth inhaled, I thought he was going to argue that he could handle more. Something in me twisted, remembering the admission he'd made to me yesterday about how he'd pushed himself too hard. But to my relief he paused and then said, "Good idea. It looks like there's a service station in a few miles."

"I'll be your trusty navigator," Naomi said, kissing her consort on the cheek. He beamed at her in return. I had to smile, watching them. She might have been nervous about how quickly they'd gotten together, but the affection between them showed in every gesture.

At the service station, Seth and Greg got out to see about the gas, and Jin immediately pulled out his paint set to create a couple more glyphs. He was working his way down the bus, the driver's area and the walls over the benches now marked. They weren't the beautiful works of art he'd turned the pendants into, but right now we were more worried about practicalities.

As Greg settled into the driver's seat and Seth sat down next to me, the pang I'd felt earlier echoed through me again. I looked around at all my consorts.

"Can I talk to you guys for a minute? In the back?"

Naomi raised her eyebrows at us but didn't comment as they followed me past the bunks to the smaller seating area at the rear of the bus. Gabriel looped his arm around my waist as we all sat in a cluster there. "What's going on, Sprout?"

"Nothing really, I just—" I met each of their gazes, one after another. "I've had to draw on my spark for a lot of magic in the last week. Which means I've drawn a lot on you when we've been together, to light it again. I just wanted to make sure you know that if any intimacy with me ever starts to feel like too much, if we're together and the energy we're creating starts to hurt or become a strain, I want you to tell me. Right away."

"Taking a little pain for you wouldn't be a problem, angel," Damon said.

I pointed a finger at him. "No. Don't even start with that. I have *five* of you—there's no reason lighting my spark should take too much out of anyone. You've been through enough pain just because of this mess with the Assembly. If I can't trust that you'll stop me before I'm adding to it..."

My voice broke, my throat abruptly choking up. Gabriel hugged me tighter, leaning his head against mine. "Hey. You can trust us to be honest with you. Right?" He shot a pointed look around the rest of the group.

"You know I'm going to be open with you," Seth said.

Ky looked a little startled. "Of course."

"It's been nothing but good so far for me," Jin said. "But if that changes, I won't hide it from you."

"Well, when you put it that way," Damon grumbled. Then his voice softened. "I won't be keeping any secrets from you, Rose."

I exhaled in a rush. "Okay. Good. I've got so much to worry about..."

"The last thing you should have to worry about is us," Gabriel filled in. "And you don't have to. We're all in this together."

* * *

"Almost there," I said, and stifled a yawn as I looked up from the digital map. I'd taken over navigating a few hours ago, in the earliest hours of the morning. Outside the windshield, the dawn was just starting to streak over the freeway ahead of us. "We're coming up on the Oregon border in a few miles."

Jin gave me a thumbs-up from the driver's seat. "So we stop at that town near the cliffs to plan our approach?"

"That's the idea." Apprehension coiled around my gut. But the enforcers hadn't made any appearances yet. I hadn't even felt their magic. Either the enchanted glyphs now dappling the entire interior of the bus had bounced any searching spells off, or our enemies weren't even searching this area for us. They might believe we were still out east.

Naomi stirred and sat up where she'd been dozing on the opposite bench. "I'll let my mom know we've made it this far safely. She pretended to be all cool about the whole thing, but I know she's worried about us."

Kyler came up from the bunks, rubbing sleep from his eyes. He stopped beside me and squeezed my shoulder. "I can take over navigation. You should be as rested as possible before we storm The Cliff, whatever the heck it is, right?"

"Let's hope there's minimal storming involved." I got up and stretched my arms. My head did still feel a little heavy. The rumble of the bus's engine and the periodic bumping of the wheels didn't make for the easiest sleeping.

I slipped past Kyler to the bunks, checking which one was unoccupied. Instead, my gaze caught on Damon's form in the one on the lower right. The curtain had drifted open a few inches, and as I watched he rolled from one side to the other, bunching his pillow under his head. His eyes were shut, but I could tell from the brisk movement and his frown that he was awake.

Sleep wasn't coming easily to him either. Maybe because of what he might be thinking he'd have to do in the possible storming ahead of us?

I eased the curtain a little farther back and climbed in next to him. Damon shifted toward the wall, his eyes opening.

"Hey," I said. "Do you mind the company?"

His lips curled up. "Never when it's you. C'mere, angel."

It was a small space, but we fit all right when he tucked his arm around me and aligned our bodies. I snuggled close, taking a moment to just enjoy the warmth of his breath tickling over my skin. But I hadn't come over just to cuddle.

"We never really talked about that last fight," I said, keeping my voice low.

"You mean when I brought out the gun?" His tone was nonchalant, but his muscles tensed.

"Yeah." I shifted my head back so I could look him in the eyes. "How are you feeling about that? Shooting those people? Or... I don't know if you've ever been in a situation like that before."

"I've had a gun on me a few times before," he said. "But I never had to shoot at anyone. Never shot at anything other than a target on the range." He was silent for a moment, his heart thudding where our chests were pressed together. "I really only wanted to stop them from using their magic. Hurt them a little. But if I killed a couple of them, I guess that makes our lives easier."

He tensed even more as he said that. I didn't think he was as blasé about the idea as he was pretending.

"I've had to think about the same thing," I said. "Some of the enforcers I've hit with my spells... I'm not sure whether I knocked them out or really hurt them. Maybe even killed some of them. It's hard to aim that carefully when I'm doing everything I can just to block them from getting at us."

"You've done a fucking good job of blocking them," Damon said.

"It doesn't feel good though, knowing that I might have killed someone. No matter what they were trying to do to us. I wouldn't ever have wanted to be a killer." Saying those words out loud made my stomach ball into a knot.

"You're not one," Damon said with a sudden fierceness. He eased his hand around my head to draw my forehead under his chin, his fingers stroking over my hair. "No one could call you that for just defending yourself and people you care about. Nothing you've done has changed the way I think about you, angel. Don't you ever worry about that."

I breathed in the bittersweet smell of him and let my lips brush the bare skin just above the collar of his T-shirt. "The same goes for you. Nothing you've done has changed the way I think about you, Damon. Or how much I love you."

He swallowed audibly. Then he was tilting my chin

up to capture my mouth with his, his kiss searingly passionate. I arched into him as the sensation flooded me. His other hand slid down to my ass, urging me against him.

"It's been too long since I've been inside you," he muttered against my lips. The words sent a fresh wave of heat through me.

I kicked the curtain completely closed. "There's an easy way to fix that."

He chuckled and cupped his hand between my legs, drawing a gasp I couldn't contain from my throat. My body thrummed with anticipation as he rolled his weight onto me. His thumb flicked open the button of my jeans.

Then feet thumped against the floor at the front of the bus, and I stiffened.

"My mom just texted me," Naomi called back to us, her voice sharp with panic. "Aunt Irene said something to her—Mom thinks Irene tipped off the Assembly. They might know where we are right now."

Damon swore. I'd barely had time to scramble out from under him when the air warbled. The bus rocked with a wallop of magic.

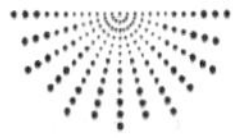

CHAPTER TWENTY-FOUR

Damon

At the first heave of the bus, Rose was shoving past the curtain to run to the front. Even as a jolt of adrenaline rushed through me, a prickle of annoyance ran alongside it. The Assembly assholes really had picked the worst time to launch their latest attack. My body ached with the loss of my woman against me.

But I didn't have time to dwell on that right now. As the bus swayed again, lurching to a stop, I pawed around the blanket for my backpack. With a yank of the zipper, my fingers had closed around the grip of the pistol. The same one I'd used earlier, although none of the other guys had decided to give firepower a try with the two others I'd picked up. It melded into my hand, leaving me with a weird mix of confidence and trepidation.

Rose's words, her murmur in my ear just a few moments ago, came back to me. If I hurt people right now, even if I killed them, she knew it was only because I had to. She knew I didn't like the idea of that kind of blood on my hands.

As long as I had her, the rest didn't matter.

"They're not managing to break through the barrier we've put up inside the bus," Naomi was saying when I hurried to join the rest of the group at the front. "The magic in the glyphs is holding for now. But we don't have anything on the outside to deflect them completely."

"And it won't hold forever," Rose said, her face drawn. "Not with a bunch of them hitting us."

"Can we just drive through them?" Kyler asked.

Rose shook her head and pointed to the windshield. Beyond the glass, several feet down the road, a glinting wall of magic rose from the asphalt.

Not just a wall. A ring. And as I watched, it contracted in on us. Shadowy figures moved behind it— directing it, I guessed. My body tensed defensively.

"What happened to keeping a low profile with their magic?" I said.

Jin grimaced in the driver's seat. "I think they redirected the other traffic to set up this ambush, the way they cleared the streets in New York that time. I thought things were just quiet because it's so early in the morning. I was just starting to think it was strange I hadn't seen any other cars in a few minutes when they hit us."

"We can't let them close in on us," Rose said. "We've got to push them back, break our way through."

The bus shook. Naomi swiveled her arms in a quick

magicking. She swore under her breath. "There's hardly enough room in here to work properly."

"We can—" Gabriel started, and the bus door wrenched open.

Two enforcers charged up the steps, magic blazing around their hands. Rose cried out and whirled with the fastest spell I'd ever seen her cast. A blast of air tossed our attackers off their feet, but there were more rushing in. A sizzling bolt of magic flew through the open doorway and smacked the back of Jin's seat.

Rose threw herself forward through the doorway, moving in the strange dance of her magic as she went. The energy she gave off let out an electric crackle. Someone on the road beyond yelped. Naomi raced after her, her face pale and her hands tight.

I wasn't letting them go out there alone. I brushed past Ky and Greg to the doorway, gun raised. Seth was already hurtling out, and Gabriel came right at my heels.

"Hold back," Gabriel said. "We don't want to get in the way of the girls' magic. Just be ready if the enforcers try to rush the bus again."

I was already swinging around, searching for those shadowy figures through the hazy shell of magic they'd pushed up around us. My finger squeezed the trigger. The bang of the shot reverberated up my arms and rang in my ears. Someone beyond that barrier flinched, clutching their arm. Good.

As I swerved to the left, Rose and Naomi let out a shout in unison. Wind rushed past me, and the magical barrier that had hemmed us in shattered. I caught one glimpse of scattered men and women on the asphalt and the grass beyond the guardrail, and then they were charging at us, hands and magically charged batons waving.

I fired two more shots, my back against the bus, and then Naomi dodged into my line of fire. Gabriel leapt in to tackle a woman near the edge of the fray. Fuck. I couldn't keep shooting when I was as likely to hit one of us as one of them.

I shoved the pistol into the back of my jeans and hurled myself into the fight. A guy with one of those glowing batons charged at me. I could tell in an instant that he wasn't used to any kind of hand-to-hand fighting. I ducked under the thrust of his baton and elbowed him in the gut.

He staggered backward. I didn't give him a second to recover. Ramming into him with my shoulder, I knocked him right to the ground. My hand lashed out and yanked the baton from his grasp, sending it rattling under the bus.

The guy tried to shove himself up and me off him, but I was faster. I whipped the pistol out and pointed it at his forehead. He froze.

Yeah. This dude didn't have any magic outside of that glorified wand to protect himself with. Nothing that would block a bullet from entering his brain. Maybe he was rethinking this whole career path he was on right now.

Shouts and sizzles of magic carried around me, but I didn't risk looking away from my captive for a second.

"Who sent you here?" I said, jamming the muzzle of

the gun against his forehead. "Tell me every name you know that's in on this mission."

The guy stared back at me with his mouth clamped tight.

"Come on," I said. "Just one or two, and maybe you'll walk away from here."

When he didn't answer, I waggled the gun. "Or you could tell me about this Cliff you all think is so important."

His eyes twitched with a flicker of panic. Huh. I leaned in, and he spat out at me, "I don't know anything about what happens at The Cliff. But even if I did, I'd let you kill me before I told you. You think there aren't worse things that could happen to me? The people I work for have been very clear."

Maybe he'd weigh his options a little differently if I started with his kneecaps. I hesitated, wondering if that was the direction I wanted to go in—if I wanted to be the kind of guy who would shoot someone lying helpless to try to get an answer from them, if I even *could* be that kind of guy—and a wave of magic resounded across the freeway with the force of a sonic boom.

It jostled me off the guy, and it sent the guy's body slamming even more solidly into the pavement. His head lolled, his muscles going limp. Not dead, I realized at the rise of his chest. Just unconscious.

"I think we knocked them all out," Rose said, spinning around. Her black hair was wild around her face. Beside her, Naomi wiped a smear of ash and blood from her cheek with the back of her hand. "Let's go—let's go! We don't know how many more might be coming."

* * *

Seth had taken a nasty blow to the temple that had left a cut seeping blood where he'd been hit in the minivan crash, and Gabriel's forearm was scorched with a magical burn. As Rose and her cousin cast their best healing spells to mend the damage and Jin set the bus roaring on down the freeway, I found myself sitting next to Greg. The first witching guy I didn't have any reason to hate. Which didn't mean I had any idea what to say to him.

"So, this is what you've been dealing with since you broke out of the Assembly prison, is it?" he said after a moment.

"Yeah. They don't know when to let up."

"They're obviously very scared of what you could tell people." He rubbed his mouth, his eyes fixed on Naomi. "It could change a lot."

"That's what Rose says," I said. "I've got to admit, I don't know a whole lot about the political side of things. I'm here for her."

One side of his mouth quirked up. "I know that feeling. Naomi wasn't going to let Rose head back into the fray alone." His gaze slid to me. "We got a couple of good ones, didn't we?"

"If by good you mean keeping our lives way too exciting," I said, but I didn't really want to joke about it. "Yeah," I added. "It looks like we did."

From Greg's expression as he turned back to watch his consort, he didn't much care how much danger she dragged him into. Well, I knew *that* feeling too.

I'd take a fighter over a pushover any day.

"Do you really think Aunt Irene tipped off the Assembly?" Rose said to Naomi as she straightened up. She left her hand resting fondly on Seth's short-cropped hair, just above the skin she'd sealed.

"I don't know," Naomi said. "My mom wasn't very clear—I didn't really have time to ask her with everything happening so fast. And now I'm kind of scared to text her anything, even talking vaguely the way I was before." She let out a sharp breath. "All I know is that she caught Aunt Irene in the house with her—my mom's—phone. Irene saw that last text from me about reaching the border. And when Mom confronted her, Aunt Irene said something that made her worried."

"Why would she *do* that?" Ky said, frowning.

Naomi's head drooped. "I don't know. Maybe in some weird way she thinks she's protecting the family. The rest of it, other than us, I mean. I'm sure she found some way to justify it to herself. But it doesn't matter. It's not as if I'm heading back home."

"You thought we could trust her," Rose said.

"I never thought she'd go this far. But I guess we've never been in a situation like this for me to know. I'm sorry."

"No!" Rose touched her cousin's arm. "I'm not blaming you. I'm just saying—I know it feels awful. Thinking you knew someone better than that. After what happened with my dad... Anyway, maybe your mom misunderstood."

Even after everything she'd been through, my angel was willing to give these people the benefit of the doubt. My hands clenched at my sides. If I had my way, after everything they'd already put her through, we'd burn all of them down—the entire Assembly, every part of this awful witching society of hers except maybe the two of them with us...

Rose turned toward me then, with a slightly pained smile that nonetheless sent a piercing sensation through me. Suddenly I was remembering her yesterday, open and vulnerable, asking us to trust her. My throat tightened.

I wanted to burn everything down, but this was her fight more than mine. And she still wanted to salvage some of this witching world. She still saw hope in it.

Maybe I could offer something more than fire, if that was what she needed.

"I tried to question the guy I tackled," I said. "He got pretty edgy when I asked about The Cliff. But I'm pretty sure he doesn't know any details. The way he was talking, there's really nothing this faction of your Assembly cares about more than keeping their secrets. He was ready to let me kill him for things he didn't even know."

Rose nodded. "If their conspiracy to steal witches' power ever got out, every member of that faction would lose everything. And we don't even know why they're doing it, what they might stand to lose there."

"Well, I'm thinking that's a whole lot of leverage right there," I said. "We don't know if we can get this proof, at least not right now. Not soon enough to save our lives. But there might be a way we can make them back off without it."

Gabriel cocked his head. "What do you mean?"

"You ever hear the term 'mutually assured

destruction'? Both sides could destroy the other, but they agree not to, to save themselves." I motioned toward the fallen bodies now far behind us on the freeway. "If we can make them believe we have enough to bring them down, we can bargain based on that. If they care that much about saving their skins, we might never need to reveal the bluff."

"I *want* to take them down, though," Rose said.

"But if we can't find enough right away to convince the rest of your society that your story is true, a deal like that could at least buy us some time," Seth said. "It's a backup plan."

"Yeah." I grinned. "So maybe it's not such a bad thing they know we're here. All we have to do is make it to that 'Cliff,' and they'll wet their pants trying to contain what we might know."

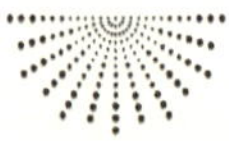

CHAPTER TWENTY-FIVE

Rose

We parked on the main street of the little town that was home to the newspaper with the article on the Frankford family's property, and within fifteen minutes Gabriel had managed to chat the exact location of that property out of someone. He tipped his head to the elderly lady he'd struck up a conversation with outside a cheese shop and ambled back to me.

"It's about five miles north up the coast," he said. "'Not much to look at,' according to her."

"If there's something important up that way, I'm sure there's some kind of protection on the property," I said. "Presumably at least partly magical."

"Which is why it's a good thing we've got two witches on our side now, huh?" he said with his usual smile, but then his gaze flicked away from me to scan our surroundings warily.

"We've better get going," I said. I waved to Naomi, who'd gone with a few of the guys to grab some food at the local café. "If that enforcer Damon questioned mentions we were asking about The Cliff, they'll be coming out here after us with guns blazing. Metaphorically."

"I'd rather deal with guns than some of the magic they've got at their disposal," Gabriel said.

We all piled back into the bus where Jin was adding a few more glyphs by the windows and Kyler was tapping away on his laptop. "I still haven't found any way to get deeper into the network from a remote link," Ky said.

"Maybe we won't even need that," Damon said, dropping onto the bench beside him. "Maybe we'll find everything we need to shut those assholes down at this cliff." He didn't sound all that optimistic.

Gabriel took the driver's seat and revved the engine. I sat down next to Naomi.

"Anyone guarding the place, any enforcers that come after us, we use the same spell we did on the freeway," I said. "Knock 'em out. All we need is to get in there, see what we can find, and get right back out."

My cousin nodded. "It worked back there." She raised one eyebrow at me. "I can understand why they're worried about you being on the loose, Rose. I've never seen any witch who can wield magic with as much force as you do. I don't know if it's the mixing of the Levesque and Hallowell genes or having five consorts supporting you or what, but they picked the wrong witch to mess with when they took you on."

I laughed haltingly. "I think that's *why* they took me

on. Why they wanted control over my magic." At least, that was what Celestine had said. I leaned my head back against the hard surface of the window behind me. "I don't know why Dad wanted to marry a Levesque in the first place if he was going to be so scared of how powerful their kids might be."

"Maybe they really were in love for a little while," Naomi said. "Like in one of those romance books. If those are even remotely accurate, people do some pretty stupid things when they're caught up in that initial rush of emotion. And then sometimes they do even stupider things if they wake up and realize their actions had more consequences than they considered."

"This should be the place up here," Gabriel said with a motion toward the windshield. "That driveway will take us—no, better not to go down there."

My head jerked around at his last words, the abrupt change in tone. At the same moment, magic tingled over my skin.

"There are wards," I said. "To divert anyone who considers coming to visit. Slow down before you reach the driveway."

I focused my attention inward, to the bonds that thrummed between me and each of my consorts. With a few twitches of my hands, I directed some of my strength through those connections into them, bolstering the defenses I'd already built around them. Adding an extra tread to dispel the compulsion of that ward more directly.

Gabriel shook his head. "That felt... really odd," he said. "We do want to go down there, right?"

"Yeah," I said. "Just keep taking it slow. I doubt those wards are the only layer of protection."

Naomi and I moved to stand next to him, peering through the windshield as we turned west toward the Frankford property. A stretch of trees hid the actual coastline, but the air the fan was pulling in from outside carried a hint of salt and wet rock. I gripped the railing by the steps. A faint quiver touched my skin.

"Stop!" I shouted. Gabriel hit the brakes. The second I had solid footing, I was whipping up the spell I'd used before, the one that seemed to smack the consciousness right out of our enemies' heads. Naomi whirled her hands beside me, propelling her magic to me to add to the heft of my casting.

A spell from outside hit the windshield, sending a crack down the middle of it. The whole thing probably would have shattered if not for Jin's painted reinforcements. A few more blasts of magic rattled the metal shell around the engine.

Before the unseen guards could throw anything at us strong enough to break down the whole bus, I hurled my spell forward. I felt rather than saw several minds go dark. A breath stuttered out of me.

"It's done," I said. "We can keep going. Let's hurry now. I'll keep watching in case there are more guards."

How many enforcers did this faction of the Assembly have at their disposal? I couldn't imagine they'd ever had to deal with a situation quite like this before. It might be the same ones coming after us over and over. Weren't they getting worn down?

Maybe they were. If they'd known exactly what they

were dealing with when they'd first imprisoned us, if they'd shored up their defenses enough then, we might not ever have escaped. And from that moment, in some ways I'd had the upper hand. That was the only reason we'd made it this far.

But if we didn't end this conflict soon, *I* was going to get worn out. And no matter how powerful I was, there were a lot more of them than of me.

We passed a tall but graying clapboard house that hardly looked like high witch society style. I wondered if the Frankfords had ever spent much time out here. If it was a place they'd rather no one asked about or tried to see, it was probably better not to put too much work into it.

The driveway skirted the line of trees and then looped around them to a small parking lot. The span of packed earth was empty—I didn't know where the guards had left the vehicles they'd come on. The edge of the cliff was visible now: a ragged line of slate-gray rock jutting beyond the sparse grass toward the foamy blue expanse of the ocean.

The sky overhead was gray as the rocks, clouds dimming the afternoon sunlight. As I stepped out, cool droplets flecked my face. I wasn't totally sure whether they were spit from above or spray the breeze had swept off the far-below waves. The crash of the surf hissed at the base of the cliff.

"Here we are," Greg said, looking around. "What now?"

With my hands raised, ready to begin a magicking, I crept to the cliff. I couldn't make out anything below except the thrashing waves against a rocky shoreline, but farther along, a notch was cut into the cliff edge.

"I think there's a path there," I said, pointing. "About half a mile farther along. It must lead down the cliff."

We hurried over with the salty wind licking over us. It might have been a pretty view on a sunny day, but today's clouds only made the scenery look ominous. The grass was so sparse I couldn't tell how well-traveled the route we were taking might be. Certainly this didn't seem like a place many people were likely to casually wander through, even without a magic spell repelling them.

As we came up on the notch I'd seen, it became clearer that it was indeed a path carved into the cliff face. A narrow ledge slanted sharply down along the otherwise stark drop. I paused at the top of it and looked at my companions.

"I have to go down. Whatever's waiting down there..." If it was the threat Gabriel's enforcer had seemed to think it was, I was better equipped to deal with it than anyone else here.

"You can't go alone," Damon said. "I'm not getting left behind."

Gabriel had turned to Ky in hushed conversation. "Why don't Damon and I go with you?" he said a moment later. "Everyone else can stand guard up here, ready to shout a warning if the enforcers launch another attack."

I glanced at Naomi. "Are you okay with that plan?" She was the one who'd be providing most of the defense if it came to that.

She nodded, her mouth set in a defiant line. "I won't

let them get past me." Greg reached to squeeze her hand, and she shot him a tight smile.

"Let's get this over with then," I said, and took the first step down the path. I wasn't letting any of my consorts act as my shield.

We picked our way along the descending ledge one by one. In no time at all, the top of the cliff and the people we'd left there disappeared from view and hearing. The warble of the wind and the roar of the surf drowned out everything else.

I only noticed the trap because I was so intent on setting my feet securely on the rough stone. A patch of rock just ahead of me shivered with a magical haze, and I stopped in my tracks, holding out my arm to halt Gabriel and Damon. Damon pulled out his pistol, but it wasn't as if he could shoot through a spell.

I studied the patch of magic, absorbing the wisps of energy it gave off into the air. Then I slid my foot forward with a sweep of my arm. The strands of the spell fractured apart and spun off into the air. The heat that wafted over me with their leaving suggested we'd have been burned to a crisp if the spell had been truly activated.

A shadow on the cliff face came into view up ahead. I eased down the last several feet to the opening of a cave, barely wide enough for me to step inside without brushing both my shoulders.

The guys squeezed in after me. A dim stream of daylight followed us down a passage about ten feet long. Our shoes rapped against the stone as we emerged into a larger cavern. Huge stalactites and stalagmites loomed from the ceiling and floor around us. Water dripped somewhere distant.

The space should have been dark and cool, but warmth emanated from a ruddy light at the far end of the cavern. Warmth and a pulse of energy so off-kilter it made my stomach turn.

I walked toward it, and nausea swelled to fill my entire abdomen. A faint whine filled my ears. My nerves started to jitter in revulsion. I still didn't understand what I was looking at, only that it was a ring of hazy reddish light on the far wall of the cave, maybe as tall as I was but high up near the ceiling, with a thinner reddish glow swirling within the ring in time with that pulsing, sickening energy.

There was something almost magical about that energy. A sense that it could be used to shape and control, the way I could use the magic I was familiar with. But this energy didn't move or taste the same at all, in some way I couldn't have explained.

It was simply something other, something unlike anything I'd ever experienced or could have put a name to. But every particle in my body was vibrating now with the deep certainty that whatever it was, it had never been meant to be here. To be part of this world in any way at all. It was simply *wrong*.

I was maybe ten feet away from it when a face appeared in the midst of that shifting glow. A face half the height of my entire body, its skin swirling with the same red glow, with gnarled features and eyes so dark they seemed to fall away into an abyss.

My legs jarred. A squeak of shock slipped from my

mouth. Behind me, Damon swore. The face turned its eyes toward me, and every drop of blood in my body turned cold.

The immense being's twisted mouth curved into a smile. For an instant, through the glowing ring around it, I caught a glimpse of a whirling red-tinged world sprawling out behind the monster—a world that wasn't any part of my own. Then the face pushed farther out into the cave, the suggestion of a clawed hand beside it, and I stumbled backward. My arms shot up defensively, but I didn't have a clue what magic could repel that... that *thing*.

A familiar and yet unexpected voice rang out in a language I didn't recognize. A barked command, several short choppy words.

The monster in the opening flinched. It made an expression that looked like a sneer and rasped a brief response that sounded disdainful, but it pulled back. In an instant, the red glow had swallowed it up as if it had never been there. My chest released from its painful contraction as my breath spilled out of me. But I didn't have time to enjoy my relief.

I spun around to face my father.

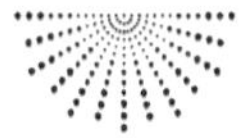

Rose

Dad had stepped out from behind one of the large stalagmites near the wall. The strange lighting of the cave made his face look haggard. My gaze shot to his hands, and mine dropped an inch from their poised position when I saw he wasn't holding any weapon. But only an inch.

"Stay right there, asshole," Damon said. *His* hands were up too, his pistol pointed directly at my dad. His face had gone sallow, I was going to guess because of the horrific visage we'd just seen, but his arms held steady.

Gabriel eased to the side, peering down the passage we'd entered through. "I don't see anyone else," he reported, his voice hoarse.

"If anyone were coming, we'd have heard from Naomi," I said. One way or another. My gaze stayed fixed on Dad, and his on me.

"They'll come," he said. "But maybe not for a while, if you got this far."

"So, you were just hanging out here waiting for us alone?" Damon said.

"I thought if we couldn't overpower you, maybe talking would get us somewhere."

"And where exactly is that?" I asked. "What are we going to talk about? How you were planning on shackling me to Derek or whatever other consort you could dig up who'd agree to your contract? What the hell that thing we just saw was? How you know how to talk to *it*?"

Dad's jaw worked. "I'm sorry, lamb," he said.

His old nickname for me hit me like a punch to the gut. He had treated me like a lamb, hadn't he? One he was going to lead to the metaphorical slaughter.

"You're *sorry*?" I repeated. "Are you fucking kidding me? Is that supposed to smooth everything over?"

He winced. "No. But it's true. I wanted to say it, before we got into anything else."

"Why did you do it?" I said. The question had been gnawing through my mind since the first moment I'd realized he was part of this scheme. "Why would you want that kind of future for me? *How could you?*"

"It wasn't that I wanted to," he said. He stayed where he was, by the wall of the cave, but he spread his hands as if in appeal. "I made a deal, one I didn't have a lot of choice in, one I didn't fully understand before I'd ever had a wife or a child... I made a deal. You felt the energy around the being that came through that portal, didn't you? You know what kind of power it has. You don't break your word when it comes to something like that."

I stared at him. "You made a deal with that thing? What does that even have to do with me and the corrupted consorting?"

"What the hell *was* that thing?" Damon broke in.

"Yeah," I said. "That too."

"We call them 'demons'," Dad said. "It must have seemed like the most appropriate word, when witching kind first summoned them. They've never really been clear on what they call themselves."

A demon. Like something out of an old story. Except the thing that had peeked into the cave—through the "portal"?—had been utterly, horrifically real.

"I don't understand," I said.

Gabriel folded his arms over his chest. "You came here to talk. Why don't you start the real explaining?"

"There isn't much to explain," Dad said. "We need magic to hold them back. We need magic to make use of them."

"And so you need to be able to force witches into doing that magic for you?" I demanded.

"It's complicated." Dad took a step toward me, and every muscle in my body tensed. "I don't want this. But we need to think of the larger consequences. You see how big this is now, don't you? How much could be at stake?"

"You could have *asked* me," I said. "You could have said you needed my help instead of trying to trick me into having no choice."

He gave me a pained smile. "No one who's had the choice has ever been much help. Rose... I tried to forget about it. I tried to pretend that everything could be normal. Everything *would* have been normal, most of the time."

"Except when you were using me the Spark only knows how."

He ignored that point. "We were counting on you," he said. "We needed you. The balance of power has already been shifting too much in their favor. The families tied to the portal can't afford to let you go, Rose. If they did, it could be catastrophic for our entire world. Not just us but all of witching society, and all of their society too." He nodded to Damon and Gabriel. "Is that what you want?"

"Don't try to turn this around on me, as if I'm somehow failing you," I said. My voice shook with a sudden surge of anger. "Don't you *dare* make this my responsibility. I still don't even know what the hell is going on. You've hardly told me anything that really makes sense."

"I've told you all you need to know," Dad said. "I need you to trust me that I wouldn't have brought you into this situation if I hadn't thought it was the only thing that would work, if I hadn't hoped I'd find a way to get you out of it again. I—"

"*Trust* you?" I sputtered, my rage flaring hotter alongside a crackle of my spark. Magic thrummed through my body, ready for my command. The man who'd raised me, who'd taught and comforted me, who'd planned to shackle me to a consort who barely tolerated me for some scheme involving the monsters behind that glowing ring—he wanted to talk about *trust*?

The hot rush of power melted my hesitation. A jolt of

resolve shot through me. My hands swiveled through the air in front of me. "I can make you tell us everything. I can drag every detail about this portal and those families—"

My compelling spell whipped through the air and disintegrated just inches from my dad. I frowned and cast again, weaving the strands even tighter. The magic I threw scattered into useless fragments around my father.

He shook his head. "You're not going to get anywhere that way. Did you think I wouldn't come prepared? You've got a lot of power, Rose, but I knew that before I came down here. I made sure I was ready for it."

He'd had other spells cast on him—repelling ones, shielding ones. I wasn't sure I believed they were layered on densely enough that I couldn't have found a way to break through them—but I also wasn't sure it would be worth the energy I'd expend finding out.

Damon waved his gun. "Are you prepared to deflect bullets?"

Dad looked at him, his gaze turning hard. "You want to shoot me? Go ahead. It isn't going to help her, if that's what you actually care about."

No, the gun wasn't a good enough threat. Not for a man who'd been willing to sacrifice his own daughter—and maybe both of his wives as well—to this conspiracy. He was far more afraid of the thing on the other side of that portal.

An idea came to me with a fresh wave of queasiness. His portal families and the Assembly resources they commandeered had gone to all this trouble to keep me alive for some purpose to do with the demons. With harnessing them. But who was to say my power couldn't be used in the opposite way.

I raised my hand toward the shifting glow on the cave wall. "Or I could try my magic on that portal. See what happens if I encourage one of your 'demons' through."

Dad's head snapped around, his face blanching. Oh, he was afraid of that, all right. "Rose," he said with a rasp. "You have no idea— For the sake of the Spark, leave that *alone*."

"Why should I?" I said, my anger flattening my voice. "Are they really going to treat me any worse than you and your associates have?"

I wouldn't, for even one second, really have considered releasing the fiend I'd seen poking its face through that opening. I could still remember the malicious inhuman energy that had wafted off it, all the way through my bones.

Dad should have known that. Dad should have known what kind of witch I was—what kind of woman I was.

But he didn't. He was staring at me with his eyes panicked-wide. He'd raised me, but he'd never paid enough attention to see who I was. To know the power I'd come into wouldn't make *me* a monster.

The last shreds of love I'd held for him crumbled into dust in that instant.

"They're evil," he said. "They'd tear you and everyone here apart. Please, Rose."

"Explain it to me," I said. "Properly. Why has this faction of the Assembly been covering up the fact that witches can take more than one consort, that we can consort with the unsparked? Where do these demons come into it? Where do *I* come into it? Make me understand." I twisted my fingers, and the portal's glow brightened. An illusion, but he couldn't tell that.

His jaw gave a nervous twitch. "I don't know all of it," he said. "I never wanted— If you ask Charles Frankford, he could tell you everything. The Frankfords have been at the center of this from the start. The Hallowells were only ever on the sidelines."

A reasonable claim. It was the Frankfords who held this land, after all. It was the current head of that household to whom Dad had turned to for advice and approval while arranging my corrupted consorting. But it wasn't as if Charles Frankford was going to sit down and have a calm, open discussion with me.

"I suppose you figure that as soon as I've left, you can warn him I'm coming, let him arrange some sort of trap," I said. I glanced at the guys. "We need his phone."

Gabriel nodded. He and Damon approached Dad, who stepped back to the wall. Dad's hands fisted. He moved to shove Gabriel away, and Damon grasped his arm, wrenching it back as he slammed his pistol to Dad's temple at the same time.

Whatever magic my father had on him didn't protect him from physical force. Dad thrashed out, but Gabriel caught his other hand, pinning it to the cave wall in turn.

"So, this is what you picked," Dad spat out as I walked up to him. "A bunch of unsparked thugs?"

Fury flared white-hot behind my eyes. I reached for the pocket where I knew Dad kept his phone and yanked it out.

"I picked love," I said, in a sharper voice than I'd known I had in me. "Maybe you could learn something from that."

The phone wasn't enough. As soon as we left, he'd be running up the cliff to that old house, and no doubt there'd be some way of contacting people in there. But I could stop him from leaving without casting a single spell directly on him.

"Leave him," I said with a gesture at the far end of the cave. Damon gave Dad a shove as he released him, sending him stumbling toward the portal.

"Rose," Gabriel said quietly, but I already knew what I had to do. I motioned them behind me, back toward the passage we'd entered through, which was the only entrance and exit this cavern possessed.

"You'll stay here with your demons until one of your 'friends' cares enough to come looking for you," I said to Dad, my hands already weaving through the air. My feet pattered out a quick rhythm on the stone floor, my arms slicing through the air, and a burst of energy surged from my spark into a wall of magic that hummed from floor to ceiling across the whole width of the cave.

Dad threw himself forward—and my wall sent him stumbling backward. He gaped at me through it.

"It'll hold at least a few days, I think," I said. "Unless someone comes down and breaks it for you first. I wonder if you matter to them even half as much as you've let them matter to you."

I spun on my heel and stalked toward the passage. Gabriel caught me with a gentle hand around my wrist.

"Rose," he said, his voice still low. "If no one comes, he could die down here."

I didn't think that was likely. The spell wasn't infinite, and there was water in that place somewhere. He wasn't going to have an enjoyable few days, that was all. But my heart was so shattered in that moment all I could say was, "Then he dies."

"And good riddance," Damon muttered.

Gabriel was silent as we tramped down the damp passage and back into the gloomy afternoon outside. When we were about halfway up the path to the top of the cliff, he dragged in a breath.

"I might have enough," he said.

I paused, glancing back at him with my hand braced against the rough rock. "What?"

He gave me half a smile. "I borrowed that phone of Ky's, the one he lifted off the enforcer, since it has an actual camera. Once I got over being scared shitless, I tried to record that—that thing with it. I don't know how well that turned out, but... I left it going after your dad started talking. He didn't admit to a whole lot, but it'll at least corroborate any other proof we find."

My spirits leapt. I would have thrown my arms around him if doing that wasn't likely to topple both of us off the cliff face.

"You're brilliant," I said.

He laughed, short and sharp. "Let's wait until we're actually out of this mess before you give me any credit."

CHAPTER TWENTY-SEVEN

Kyler

Rose lowered her hands from where she'd been weaving magic in front of my face. A light tingling had penetrated my skin, but otherwise I couldn't feel any effects. From the way she was looking at me, though, the effects were obviously there. Her expression was an odd mix of satisfied and revolted.

"I think that's as good as I can make the illusion," she said. "Considering I only had a few memories and photographs to go on."

Jin hunkered down on the bench next to her, eyeing me from the other side of the parked tour bus. "A real work of art, Briar Rose. I'd never know it was Ky, that's for sure. He looks completely like that Frankford guy to me."

"You've only ever seen the pictures." Rose bit her lip.

"I can't give you the way he moves, Ky, or his voice—I don't have enough material for that even if I knew how to. But if you stay quiet and act confident, you should be able to fool people at least for a little while." She paused. "Are you sure you want to do this?"

I heard the love running through her concern, but the question pricked at me a little anyway, even though my own nerves were jittering. I was the computer guy, the one who fought his battles from behind a screen and a keyboard. Maybe I wasn't cut out for a mission on the ground.

But we didn't have a whole lot of choice. Someone needed to go into Charles Frankford's home and find whatever records he'd have stashed there. I was the only one who could crack the security he'd have on his home computing system once we got in. I'd already determined there was no network extending outside the house that I could even try to hack into.

So I'd just have to be cut out for this mission.

"It's either me or no one," I said. "And we need any proof he can give us. We'd better get moving, right? We don't know when your dad might pass on a warning."

Rose nodded. We'd used her dad's phone to send a couple of messages to Frankford, confirming he was in Seattle at the moment, not on his country estate a couple hours outside the city. Rose figured he was more likely to keep any sensitive information in his primary estate anyway.

But without any warning, the house shouldn't be that carefully guarded. He had no reason to expect us to target him. He didn't even know I'd found those messages between him and Rose's dad, let alone that Mr. Hallowell had pointed us straight at him.

And to distract the enforcers even more, we were going to send a decoy. Naomi and Greg came over from the old minivan they'd managed to find for our purposes. Except it didn't look like a minivan anymore—in the time while Rose had been casting her illusion on me, Naomi had magicked the minivan to look like a taxi. We were parked on the side of a country road about halfway between the city and Frankford's estate.

"We take the bus into the city and get ourselves noticed near the Assembly, right?" Naomi said. "How long do you need us to keep up the distraction?"

"I don't want you getting caught," Rose said. "Be subtle about it—they'll be keeping a close watch for us anyway. And ditch the bus as soon as you can tell they're onto you. That'll convince them we're in the city for sure. If you don't use any magic after that, they shouldn't have an easy time tracking you. I'll get in touch as soon as I know what we're doing next." She managed a slight smile. "Maybe I'll be telling you we've already transmitted the damning information to every other witching family in the country."

That was the end point of our plan. Get some files from Frankford that gave a larger scope and more details on the conspiracy Gabriel's recording hinted at, then send them to every witching person on Rose and Naomi's combined Contacts list. All set up and ready to go—the second we had the files, we could send them off.

"Let's get moving then," Gabriel said. "They might already be tracking the illusion you just cast on Ky."

The gravel on the road rattled under our shoes as we hustled to the minivan. Gabriel hopped into the driver's seat, Rose beside him. I squeezed into the middle seat.

Seth dropped into the seat next to me. His gaze lingered on me. "It is really weird seeing you like that."

I laughed. "What's even weirder is I don't feel any different."

"I guess that's good." My twin hesitated and then knuckled my shoulder lightly. "You look after yourself in there, all right? I'm sure you can handle it. Treat it like it's a video game. You've beaten enough of those."

I rolled my eyes at him with a smile. "Thanks for the pep talk. I do occasionally venture out into the real world without causing any catastrophes."

"I know." His expression turned even more serious than was usual for Seth. "You're the smartest guy I know, Ky. If anyone can get past these people, it's you."

He had to be itching to take on that responsibility himself. Seth wasn't good at letting other people head into the line of fire while he hung back. I gave him a light nudge with my knee. "I promise to be careful and not do anything you wouldn't do."

That got me the chuckle I was looking for. "I hope you do a whole lot of things I *couldn't* do," he retorted.

The minivan slowed as we got close to the estate. "You'll need to roll down the window and give the security camera a look at you," Rose said. "Gabriel, park right inside. As long as we're not here too long, the employees should buy that Frankford asked the taxi to wait for him."

"Just popping in to pick up an important document I needed," I murmured, as much to myself as to confirm to them I remembered this part of the plan. I was going to have to do a little talking. The trick would be keeping it to a minimum.

When we stopped at the gate, I rolled down the window on cue. My throat tightened as the camera whirred to point at my face. But no one came running out yelling about imposters. The gate hissed open, and we were in.

Rose turned to clasp my hand. "We'll be right here waiting for you," she said. "Grab whatever you can quickly and then get out of there."

I gave her what I hoped looked like a confident smile, ignoring the pounding of my heart. "Not a problem."

The thump of my feet against the drive sounded way too loud, but no one reacted oddly to that either. Move confidently, act like I owned this place, I reminded myself. Because as far as any of the staff who saw me knew, I did. I gripped the briefcase I'd stashed my tools in and marched onward.

The door opened as I reached the front steps, and my pulse stuttered. A tall skinny man I assumed was some sort of butler stood on the other side.

"Master Frankford," he said. "We weren't expecting you today."

I pitched my voice low and gruff, as if I had a bit of a cold, and coughed a couple times for good measure. "Left something behind. Just popping in to grab it."

He glanced past me to the taxi down the drive. My body tensed. But he just nodded and stood back by the door as I strode in, his expression bland. Hopefully Charles Frankford wasn't usually the most gregarious of guys, because I wasn't going to be making small talk while I was here.

I did have to appear to have some idea where I was going. "Has my office been cleaned recently?" I said in the same rough voice.

The butler's gaze darted to the stairs. Okay, so Frankford's office was on the second floor, to the right it looked like. That gave me a decent start.

"I believe so, sir," he said.

"Good."

I strode up the stairs without looking back, forcing my hand not to grip the banister too tightly. What would Frankford's people even do to me if they realized I was an imposter?

Better not to think about that. So far, so good.

On the second floor, I found myself faced with an open landing lined with a few doors on either side. None of them screamed *office* at me. But no one else was around up here. I could do a little trial and error.

The first door I tried opened into a bedroom. The second, the knob jarred. My heartbeat kicked up another notch. Rose had said the office would probably be locked magically. Thankfully she'd given me a little tool to deal with that. Frankford would have had a bespelled key. I had a bespelled stick that was going to serve the same purpose.

As I glanced around, a cleaning woman ducked out of

one of the rooms farther down the hall. I coughed into my hand as if I had a sudden tickle in my throat. To my relief, she scurried on into the next room over without a word to me.

I palmed the stick from my pocket and poked the end of it into the keyhole. The magic Rose had imbued it with shuddered through my fingers as it expelled into the door. The air quivered in turn. And the deadbolt rasped over. A smile crossed my face.

Frankford hadn't bargained for a foe like my consort when he'd come after us.

I eased open the door and shut it behind me the moment I'd crossed the threshold. The office was all modern chic: glossy black shelving units and desk, bold geometric pattern on the rug. The desk was bare except for a small notepad and a pen holder, but an external hard drive sat on one of its side shelves. Ah ha.

I sank into the desk chair and popped open my briefcase on the desk. With the click of a couple of cables, I'd hooked the hard drive up to my laptop. I tapped my foot against the floor as it loaded.

Several of the folders I could see were password protected. With my fingers racing over the keyboard, I'd broken into them in a matter of seconds. But all I found were financial transactions that didn't look especially incriminating. A bead of sweat slid down the back of my neck as I dug deeper into the drive's files.

There was something else here. Hidden folders that no one was supposed to even realize existed, that no one was supposed to find unless they'd already known to look for them. Most people wouldn't have noticed the subtle signs.

I poked and prodded at that elusive segment. If I could just get a grip on it, carve my way in...

There. I let out a ragged breath and flicked through the contents of the folder I'd just snapped open. My eyes widened. Meeting minutes—names—discussions about The Cliff and what use to make of the demonic presence there. Files on witches who'd been roped into "helping" control those demons. Jackpot.

I didn't have time to do more than skim the first few pages. Almost giddy, I fumbled to send the entire folder straight to Rose's tablet which she'd have at the ready in the minivan. I'd already set up my phone as a wifi hotspot and connected the laptop to its signal...

But the signal was dead. I frowned and typed a few commands. Nothing. I pulled out my phone and winced at the visual on the screen—not even one bar. *No service.*

Shit. Frankford must have some kind of shielding, magical or technological, around this room—maybe even around the whole house—to cut off cellular signals from outside. No wonder I hadn't been able to detect his home network from afar. No one could sneak in, and no one could sneak his files out.

Unless they simply picked them up and carried them.

I considered grabbing the hard drive and stuffing that straight into my briefcase, but my gaze settled on a glyph marked on its top. Damon and Rose had told us about a book of incriminating notes that had burst into flames when they'd tried to take it out of the owner's house, back when we'd simply been trying to prove what her stepmother had planned for her consorting. I couldn't take the chance that Frankford had left a similar self-destruct mechanism on this drive.

My hands whipped across the keyboard to transfer the files onto my laptop. The copy progress bar crept along way too slowly for comfort.

A hand rapped on the office door. "Master Frankford," the butler called in. "There's a call for you on the home line. A representative from the Justice division named Compton."

Why was the Justice division calling here, now? I couldn't worry about that. I just had to keep going.

There was no chance anyone would believe I was Frankford if all they had was my voice, no visual to distract them. I coughed into my hand.

"I'm just finishing up here. I'll call back on my cell in the taxi."

"Do you already have her number, then?"

"Yes, I do."

He seemed to buy it. His footsteps whispered away. The progress bar crept and crept and—there, it was finished copying.

I shut down the hard drive, disconnected the cable, and stuffed all of my gear back into the briefcase. It was done. I'd done it. This whole crazy mission was almost over.

My fingers curled tight around the handle of the briefcase. I strode out into the hall and down the stairs. Confident, calm. Like I belonged here. Not like I was dying to bolt for the front door and the car waiting beyond it.

My feet had just hit the floor at the bottom of the stairs when a sound carried in from out front that made my blood run cold.

The rising rumble of several car engines converging around the estate.

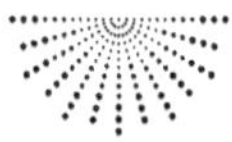

CHAPTER TWENTY-EIGHT

Rose

At the growl of engines behind us, I jerked around in my seat. Beyond the iron bars of the fence, so much like our gate on the Hallowell estate back home, a squad of navy blue cars was roaring into view. Shouts carried from other directions around the estate. My pulse hiccupped with a jolt of fear.

"What's happening?" Seth said, shifting in his seat. At the same moment, the front door of the house burst open and Kyler, still with the illusion of Frankford's face and build on him, dashed down the front steps. I wouldn't have been completely sure it was him if I hadn't felt his own panic through the consort bond between us.

"Start the engine!" I said to Gabriel, but the words had barely left my mouth when figures charged around the sides of the house toward Ky. Enforcers.

"No!" I shoved the door open, my heartbeat

thundering in my skull so loud I hardly heard the yells for Ky to stop or the screech of tires coming to a sudden stop just outside the gate. Our cover was blown, clearly. But if I could just get us out of here—

One of the enforcers thrust a blast of magic at Ky that made him stagger, the illusion shattering. He shot a panicked look at another enforcer just steps away and whipped back his arm to hurl the briefcase he was carrying toward me. "It's all on there!" he shouted.

An instant later, the enforcer tackled him to the ground with her arms and a burst of magic. The briefcase landed with a thud by my feet. I was too busy summoning a spell to try to fend off Ky's attackers to reach for it, but Jin scrambled out of the minivan and grabbed it.

"Here!" Gabriel said, holding out his hands. Jin tossed it to him and ducked back inside.

"Whatever Ky found, get it ready to send," I said. The rush of wind I sent at the enforcers who'd surrounded him only made them stumble. Not enough for him to break free.

I gathered all my focus onto the spell that had knocked them out before, but a fresh attack came from behind, searing hot bolts raining down on us. I cried out and swept out my arms to create a magical shield around the minivan. Damon had leapt out, pistol in hand, firing into the crowd of enforcers who were pushing past the opening gate.

More magic battered the shield. I couldn't do anything except keep summoning more energy of my own to bolster it. If I let down my guard for an instant, it might crack. Even as it was, a sliver of a spell pierced through and struck Damon in the hand, scorching his fingers and warping the gun.

He yelped and gripped the trigger, but the pistol didn't fire. With a muttered curse, he charged at the nearest enforcer and slammed the pistol at her head.

I cried out, too late. The enforcer fell at Damon's blow, but he'd stepped outside my shield. Three more fell on him, sharp strands of magic tightening around him. Another huge spell battered my magical barrier. My spark pinched as I threw out more energy to hold it in place.

If I stopped working on the shield to try to break Ky and Damon free, I might lose the rest of us to the enforcers. They might not have wanted to risk killing us before, but they didn't seem to care much now. They just wanted to stop us. Apparently I wasn't quite as essential to the portal families' plans as Dad had suggested.

"Halt!" a voice rang out. The battering of spells eased off. I spun around, raising my hands to launch into a new magicking.

A steel-gray-haired man in a trim suit stood in the midst of the enforcers by the gate. He shook his head at me. "I wouldn't do that."

Charles Frankford. A grim smile stretched across his angular face. "We have two of your consorts," he added. "Make another move and you'll have two fewer than you did before."

Several other figures I recognized came up beside him. The hawkish man who'd been with the enforcers in Manhattan, who'd come to interview Aunt Ginny.

Frankford's wife, Helen, who had her arms poised as if she'd been helping with the magical attack—and maybe she had. And then other witches and their consorts from among Dad's associates.

It wasn't just their squad of enforcers who'd come out to stop me. The families themselves—the ones tied to that awful portal, I had to assume—had arrived to defend their secret.

"I have the files," Gabriel said from inside the minivan. "They're ready to send to the full list. Just give me the word."

Frankford's expression tightened. "If you spread even one document you've stolen from my home, you can watch your consorts die right now."

One of the enforcers pinning Damon to the ground produced a bespelled baton from his belt and held it to Damon's temple. Across the yard, an enforcer squatting over Ky formed a searing bolt of magic in her hand, aimed over Ky's heart. My breath stopped in my chest. I held out my hand to motion for Gabriel to wait.

"If you kill them, we have no idea how that could affect me," I said. "I thought you wanted me alive and at least somewhat functioning."

Frankford folded his arms over his narrow but solid chest. "If you send out those files, whether we have you or not won't matter anymore. You ruin us, and you'd better believe we will ruin you. You and every member of your family—your cousins, your aunts—and every one of your consorts as well. I might even enjoy observing what happens to a witch who loses not one but five recent consorts, one by one."

I swallowed thickly. After seeing how brutally his people and their enforcers had attacked us this time, after witnessing the magnitude of the secret they were defending, I believed him. He would see all of us dead if he could. Spark save me, what was I supposed to do?

"Don't worry about me," Damon yelled, his voice muffled against the grass. "Do what you've got to do. Burn them all down, angel."

If only it were that simple. The enforcer on him jabbed his head with that baton, and Damon sucked in a pained breath. I flinched.

I'd brought my consorts, my cousins, everyone into this conflict. If it'd been just my life, maybe I would have made the sacrifice to expose what Charles Frankford, my father, and the rest of them had done, but I couldn't give up on everyone else I cared about. There had to be another way.

My thoughts tripped back to something else Damon had said, after the last time we'd faced off against this faction. Mutually assured destruction. The threat of exposure was plenty of leverage all on its own. I didn't even know for sure if what Ky had found was enough to completely destroy Frankford's group and what they'd been doing, but the Frankfords obviously thought it could be. That was all I needed to shift the balance.

I turned back to Charles Frankford, my chin high. "If you attack us again, my consort will send the files we found to every witching family in North America. If we expose you, you'll kill us. We're at a bit of a standstill, aren't we? What if we made a deal that gets us both out of this mess?"

Frankford cocked his head, looking skeptical. "I'm listening."

"We could make a binding oath," I said. "We both agree to the conditions, and we both accept magical compulsion to follow them, to ensure we don't break that contract."

"What 'conditions' would you want?" Helen Frankford asked. Her pale eyes were icy.

I kept my gaze on her and her husband, but at the corner of my eye I saw Damon squirm, the enforcer jab him again, the spasm of pain running through his body. My jaw tightened. I had to think carefully, clearly—not let my emotions rush me. If this was going to work, if it was really going to protect me and my loved ones, I had to construct the terms of the binding perfectly.

"I will swear that I and my consorts will not share or speak of the files we obtained with anyone. In return, I ask that you swear to ensure that no harm comes to me, my consorts, or my family from you or any families or Assembly employees associated with you, by your hand or at your orders. We must be absolved of any criminal charges currently active against us. And I want to be named the official head of the Hallowell estate."

"And your father?" Frankford said dryly.

I shrugged. "I don't want to see him again, but he can stay in the Portland house if he wants. He can keep his personal account. The rest is mine." There wasn't any point in taking everything from him. That would only make him even more my enemy. Right now, all I wanted was peace.

Frankford looked uncertain. I didn't want to give *him* too much time to think.

"I'm being generous," I said. "I could have the files sent right now, if you're unwilling to negotiate."

I moved my hand toward Gabriel, and Helen Frankford raised hers to stop me. "We'll discuss it," she said. "We can't swear to a binding we don't all agree on."

"Be quick," I said. "Five minutes. Then the files go out."

"I'm ready," Gabriel said quietly.

The Frankfords gathered with the other families to consult. I waited, my body still braced to call forth more magic if I needed it, my heart thumping behind my ribs. My mind raced through the possibilities, trying to figure out if I'd left open any loopholes. Even one word out of place in the final oath, and they could still find a way to hurt us.

Of course, the same was true for us hurting them.

I caught Gabriel's eye and glanced from the laptop to the tablet he'd left propped between the seats. "We want to be ready for any possibility," I said.

A glint that looked like understanding lit in his eyes. He shifted his hand just slightly, opening up a new window on the computer.

The families had finished their discussion. Charles Frankford motioned to the minivan. "You will guarantee that neither you nor anyone else who's aware of those files will make any mention of them or pass even a piece of them on to anyone else?" he said.

I nodded. "I'll swear to that."

"I take it the files were transferred onto that

computer you have there. We also want them wiped from its hard drive."

Exactly as I'd suspected they'd ask. "All right," I said.

"And you'll make no accusations against our families, including your father. You won't speak of what you've learned here at all."

I hesitated.

"Rose," Damon protested. "You can't let them get away with all this shit."

My stomach twisted. I glanced at Gabriel, and he gave me a slight tip of his head. Not that the measure I hoped he'd taken would make a lot of difference once we'd sworn the oath. But it was something.

If I agreed to the Frankfords' terms, all those other witches who'd been trapped in the portal families' schemes, or who might be trapped later—I was abandoning them. But I couldn't protect them and my consorts at the same time. My first loyalty had to be to the five men I loved and had sworn not to harm.

"I'll accept those terms," I said. "As long as you also swear that you'll do everything in your power to ensure no further criminal charges are brought against us."

The Frankfords exchanged a glance with the other families. Helen pursed her lips.

"All right," she said. "There's also the matter of your unusual consorting. You'll make no mention of that to anyone in witching society. And your consorts must make no mention of magic to any unsparked party."

"We wouldn't anyway," Gabriel said.

I'd bristled. "I won't go shouting about my consorting," I said. The Spark only knew what most of the more liberal witches would think of it, even. "But if I'm asked, I've got to be able to say something. People will be even more suspicious if I can't say anything, and I'm not going to agree to telling a total falsehood."

She studied Gabriel and the laptop he was holding for a moment.

"Time's almost up," I said, hoping I sounded less terrified than I felt. "I can give him the word right now."

Charles Frankford grimaced at his wife. "Fine," he said to me. "Then you won't volunteer the information. Do we have a deal?"

I exhaled some of the tension I'd been holding in. "We do. Shall we construct the binding oath together, then?" My gaze slid back to Helen Frankford.

"Let's get this over with," she said briskly. At a flick of her fingers, the enforcers holding Ky and Damon dragged the guys over. I waved the other three out of the minivan. Gabriel, Seth, and Jin stood around me as the portal families clustered together across from us. Gabriel still clutched the laptop.

I weaved my hands through the air as Helen Frankford did, summoning all the power of my spark into the spell. It had to be solid and unwavering to bind them securely. Since we were creating it together, we'd both be building it strong, to prevent the other side from slipping loose.

The strands of magic hummed through the air, around me and my consorts, around the Frankfords and their associates. I spoke up first.

"If Charles and Helen Frankford and the families that stand with them swear that they will do and order no harm—to our lives, our freedom, or our happiness—to me, Rose Hallowell, any man bound to me as consort, and any member of my family, Hallowell or Levesque; that all criminal charges against us will be dropped and they will do everything in their power to prevent further ones being made; and that the inheritance of the Hallowell estate will now pass to me, then I too swear that my consorts, my family, and I will not spread the files we discovered or word of them, and will remove them from this computer; we will not speak of the criminal activities of the Frankfords, Maxim Hallowell, or their associates that we have learned about in the past month; and I will not volunteer information about my consorting, nor will my consorts speak to other unsparked parties about magic."

Helen Rockford raised her voice in return. "As Rose Hallowell swears that she, her consorts, and her family will wipe the files they stole from the computer they loaded them onto and make no mention or transfer of them to any other party; that they will not speak of the crimes they've learned in relation to my family and my associates; and that she and her consorts will be circumspect about the nature of their consorting, so I, Helen Rockford, and the families that stand with me swear that we will do and order no harm to the lives, freedom or happiness of Rose Hallowell, any man bound to her as consort, or her family; that we will see them absolved of any current criminal charges and do our best to prevent any future ones; and that the Hallowell estate will now pass to her."

"So we swear," we said together, and our voices

crackled with the charged words. The spell whirled around us and tingled into my skin. I felt the hold of it clamp around my mind for a fleeting second before the sensation faded away.

Gabriel shuddered beside me. Then his fingers moved as if on autopilot to cancel the email he'd been poised to send and then to trash the files.

Frankford held out his hands. "I think we'll just take that."

"And release her consorts," Helen Frankford said to the enforcers.

The ones who'd been restraining Ky and Damon stepped back. Damon glowered at them and rubbed his arms. Ky made a strained noise as Gabriel handed over his computer.

"Well, I hadn't gotten it that customized yet," he said as if consoling himself.

"Back in the car," I said to the guys, and motioned to the figures gathered around the gate. "Why don't you clear the way?"

Frankford looked up from the computer and smiled thinly. At a gesture from his wife, the group of enforcers parted.

"There," he said, in a tone that didn't sound victorious or defeated. "Go on home, Rose Hallowell. And the Spark willing, our paths will never cross again."

I returned his smile as I opened the front passenger door. "Nothing would make me happier."

CHAPTER TWENTY-NINE

Rose

It'd been less than two weeks since I'd last set foot inside the manor, but somehow stepping into the wide foyer of my family home with the crystal chandeliers overhead and the curving wooden staircase ahead of me, breathing in the smells of old wood and recent polish, I felt as if I'd arrived somewhere unfamiliar. Maybe because this was the first time I'd been able to walk through those doors with my consorts at my side.

"It's probably not a good idea for us to *stay* here, right?" Kyler said, looking around. "All the time, I mean."

"If we want to avoid a whole lot of talk from people in town, it's probably better if we mostly use Seth's house," I said. "But I want you to feel like this is your home too. It's the weekend. Hardly any staff are around. After everything we've been through, I think I deserve one night with you here."

Jin took in the place with a grin. "I can agree to that."

I made a shooing gesture. "For now, poke around. Get comfortable. There are half a dozen guest rooms if you want to pick one we can make yours. Nothing's off limits. Before anything else, *I* am going to take a shower." It'd been too long since my last one, and my skin still felt gritty from that scramble down the cliff face.

Upstairs, I hesitated in the hall. Technically the master bedroom that had once been my dad's and Celestine's was now my domain. The thought of stepping in there to the ghosts of their presences made me shiver.

I eased open the door and peeked inside. My stance relaxed. Before we'd left, I'd asked one of the cleaning staff to change the bedding. The sheets and duvet were crisply laid out, nothing about them suggesting anyone else had ever slept here. Celestine had swept her belongings off the dresser before she'd left under my compulsion. The bedroom window had been left open, a light breeze stirring the gauzy curtains. The room smelled like the summer flowers blooming outside, fresh and sweet.

If I was going to take over as lady of the house, I had to start somewhere.

I grabbed my bath supplies from the common bathroom and carried them to the master bedroom's en-suite. I was just checking that the towels were fresh too when the floor creaked by the doorway.

"Hey," Damon said, poking his head in. "How'd you like some company?"

I raised an eyebrow at him, and he grinned in response.

"I could use a shower too, you know," he added.

"Oh, and I'm sure that's the only reason you're looking for an invitation."

"Well, no." He sauntered over to me and looped his arms around my waist. His breath tickled my ear as he spoke. "I believe we started something in the bus a couple nights ago that we still haven't finished."

His touch was enough to send desire spiking up from my belly. "You make a good point. But I do still want to shower."

"Oh, I was counting on that."

He slid his hands to the hem of my shirt and tugged it over my head. His gaze darkened with hunger as he took in the swell of my breasts within my bra. Reaching to unclasp it, he leaned in for a kiss at the same time. I soaked in the heat of his mouth, need tingling through me, and ran my hands down his chest. With a yank, I removed his shirt in turn.

My fingers settled on the bulge beneath the fly of his jeans. I pressed against it teasingly, and Damon growled. He stripped my jeans and panties off me and nudged me up against the glass wall of the shower stall.

"Shower first," I reminded him, breathless.

"You'd better hurry up and get me undressed then, huh?"

I wasn't going to wait for an even more explicit invitation. I unzipped his fly, and he stepped out of his jeans, kicking his boxers after them. My rebel had an impressive body I hadn't gotten the chance to admire in a while. I traced my fingers over the taut muscles from shoulders to abdomen, noting the little scars here and there. His cock stood at attention between us, thick and hard. Heat pooled between my legs at the thought of taking him into me.

Soon, but not yet. I turned on the water and pulled him with me into the warm spray.

Damon kissed me again as the water cascaded over us, his hands slicking up and down my arms and then cupping my breasts.

"Let's get you clean," he said in a meltingly low voice.

As I shampooed my hair, he soaped up his hands and ran them over my body again, gliding with that slippery sheen. Everywhere he touched, desire flared beneath my skin. He swivelled his palms against my nipples and then dipped his fingers over my clit down to my opening. A moan tumbled out of me.

But I could pay back that torture. I grabbed the soap and spread suds across that well-muscled body, all the way down to his erection. Gripping it tightly, I stroked him up and down until he pressed me up against the shower wall again.

"I'm fucking sparkling now, and so are you, angel. Time to get to the good stuff."

No argument here. I smacked the lever down to shut off the water.

Damon scooped me off my feet, bracing me against him with my core flush against his cock, as he shoved the glass door open. He carried me across the room, and we toppled together onto the bed side by side. Our skin was still damp, but I didn't want to wait any more than he did.

He hooked one of my legs over his hip and drove into me. His cock stretched me with a burn so sweet I couldn't hold back another moan.

I didn't have to. There was no one in the house right now I had to hide my joy from.

We rocked together like that, facing each other on our sides. Damon brushed the damp strands of my hair away from my eyes and kissed me hard. Then he just stared into my eyes as his thrusts sped up, taking me deeper and deeper with every one. But the look in his eyes was so tender it made my heart ache. Pleasure rippled through me, filling me, lifting me.

I grasped his shoulders, trying to hold on, to keep that connection, but he plunged against the sweet spot inside me and my eyes rolled back of their own accord. My orgasm rushed through me with a bliss both demanding and loving. I cried out, arching toward him, and he groaned as he spilled himself inside me.

He stayed there as his cock softened, gathering me even more tightly against him. I tipped my head against his chest. His fingers grazed over my hair in a gentle caress.

"I meant it, you know," he said.

"What?" I said, my lips brushing his naked skin, his bittersweet scent filling my lungs.

"When they had me, out at that guy Frankford's house. When I told you to do what you had to do. I'd never want you to give up what matters to you for me. If I ever go down, it'll be my own fault. Don't you hold yourself back for me. All right?"

"Damon."

He pulled back to look me in the eyes again. "All *right*?"

I grimaced at him. "*You* matter to me. I'm not going to give this up."

He didn't look completely satisfied, but he tucked his head over mine again.

The door whispered open. "Ah," Jin's voice said, teasing. "Getting started without the rest of us, are you?"

Damon huffed. "Not my fault if the rest of you didn't take the same initiative. Plenty of room here. What are you waiting for?"

I laughed as not just Jin but all four of my other consorts hopped onto the bed around us.

"Group hug?" Kyler said, and Gabriel chuckled. I just sighed and nestled happily among the men I loved.

* * *

Sometime in the middle of the next morning, I wandered into the front yard where I'd spotted Gabriel from the window. He was standing by the garage, eyeing the row of parking spots, most of them now empty. I wondered if Dad would be by to pick up his other cars or if he was going to abandon them to my use. At some point I'd have to pick out one of my own, I supposed.

"You know, I don't think it makes any sense for you to stay a Hallowell employee," I told Gabriel, coming up beside him. "Paying you to work for me would feel really weird at this point."

He slung his arm around me. "I can see that. Just as

long as you'll let me freeload in the garage apartment. And I should probably keep tinkering with the cars, for appearances and so I don't die of boredom."

I rolled my eyes. "So, you're going to be working for me *without* me paying you? I'm not sure that's better."

He grinned and leaned in to give me a quick kiss. "I like the tinkering. I like the apartment. It'll keep the rumors in check, right? I promise I won't do any oil changes or engine maintenance I don't want to."

"I guess that's all right then," I grumbled.

He laughed and nuzzled my cheek. Then a shadow passed through his bright blue eyes.

"We're not leaving things here, are we? Just spending the rest of our days relaxing around the estate and pretending we're not in one epically big relationship? Those... demons, and all the other witches Frankford and your father and the others might be hurting because of them..."

My chest tightened. "I know," I said. "Believe me, I haven't really stopped thinking about that. I promised not to share the files or talk about what we learned, but there have to be other ways I can take down the families involved with the portal without breaking the contract we agreed to. I should probably start by reading through those files so I know exactly what we're up against. You've still got them on your tablet."

Gabriel nodded. "I can shoot them over to your computer whenever you need them. Probably better if we have multiple copies, just in case."

"And we have the video you took, which they didn't

even know about to include it in the binding." I nibbled at my lower lip. "It'll take some maneuvering, but we're going to keep fighting. You can count on that. I just want to take the time to do it smart, now that I have a little breathing room. We were on the run too long."

The rumble of an engine made my shoulders tense. I peered through the gate as a small dented Ford eased up outside. It wasn't the kind of posh vehicle I'd have expected an Assembly member to be driving, but I couldn't take that as a guarantee.

A woman who didn't look much older than me stepped out on the driver's side. Her fawn-brown hair was scattered around her face, her rectangular glasses askew. She pushed them farther up her nose and caught sight of us through the bars. Her body went rigid and then relaxed, just slightly.

"Is this the Hallowell estate?" she said in a soft raspy voice.

I stepped forward, Gabriel following behind me. "It is," I said. "I'm Ro—I mean, Lady Hallowell. Can I help you?"

She hugged herself, but a small bright smile touched her face. "I hope so," she said. "Your cousin Naomi sent me this way? I was told this is a safe place for witches who... who can't trust the people they thought they could."

I blinked at the young woman. Where had Naomi come up with that? We hadn't discussed anything like this.

Then a smile of my own curved my lips. Whatever my cousin had been thinking, she'd been right.

"It *is* a safe place," I said, moving to open the gate. "Why don't you come in and tell us why you're here? And then we'll see what we can do to make everything out there safer too."

ABOUT THE AUTHOR

Eva Chase lives in Canada with her family. She loves stories both swoony and supernatural, and strong women and the men who appreciate them. Along with the Witch's Consorts series, she is the author of Their Dark Valkyrie series, the Dragon Shifter's Mates series, Demons of Fame Romance series, the Legends Reborn trilogy, and the Alpha Project Psychic Romance series.

Connect with Eva online:
www.evachase.com
eva@evachase.com

www.ingramcontent.com/pod-product-compliance
Lightning Source LLC
Chambersburg PA
CBHW021308190726

48288CB00003B/750